Vasudeva's Family

Vasudeva's Family

Asprushyaru

VAIDEHI

Translated from Kannada by
Susheela Punitha

Edited by
Mini Krishnan

OXFORD
UNIVERSITY PRESS

Oxford University Press is a department of the University of Oxford.
It furthers the University's objective of excellence in research, scholarship,
and education by publishing worldwide. Oxford is a registered trademark of
Oxford University Press in the UK and in certain other countries

Published in India by
Oxford University Press
YMCA Library Building, 1 Jai Singh Road, New Delhi 110 001, India

© Oxford University Press 2012

The moral rights of the author have been asserted

First Edition published in 2012

All rights reserved. No part of this publication may be reproduced, stored in
a retrieval system, or transmitted, in any form or by any means, without the
prior permission in writing of Oxford University Press, or as expressly permitted
by law, by licence, or under terms agreed with the appropriate reprographics
rights organization. Enquiries concerning reproduction outside the scope of the
above should be sent to the Rights Department, Oxford University Press, at the
address above

You must not circulate this book in any other form
and you must impose this same condition on any acquirer

ISBN-13: 978-0-19-808961-2
ISBN-10: 0-19-808961-9

MR. Omayal Achi MR. Arunachalam Trust was set up in 1976 to further
education and health care particularly in rural areas. The MR. AR Educational
Society was later established by the Trust. One of the Society's activities is to
sponsor Indian literature. This translation is entirely funded by the
MR. AR Educational Society as part of its aims.

Typeset in Aldine 401 BT 10/13.4
by Eleven Arts, Keshav Puram, Delhi 110 035
Printed in India at Rakmo Press, New Delhi 110 020

May the earth truly be one family through our endeavour;
may we make the ideal *Vasudhaiva Kutumbakam*
a reality in our communities

Contents

Author's Note	ix
Translator's Note	xiii
Introduction	xv
Kinship Terms	xxxi
1. A Birth	1
2. Parthakka	14
3. Bhaskara	32
4. Black Magic	38
5. Ramayana in the Attic	47
6. Rathna's Husband	53
7. Sheena	60
8. The Namakarana	67
9. The Koosa Woman	75
10. Vasudevaraya	86

11. Genda	93
12. Marriageable Girls	102
13. The Headlines	112
14. Thukri aka Kumudhini	119
15. Another Birth	125
An Autobiographical Note	130
Glossary	144

Author's Note

I am a home-grown writer; my Kannadiga world-view was formed by the elders of my family. It began in the inner rooms of our house, a home filled with adults and children of almost every size and variety; from their responses to the joys and sorrows that came our way.

In a house with babies, a lullaby like this one was a constant drone:

Why are you crying, my sweet little one?
You have everything you need.
When you ask, I'll give you frothy milk from four buffaloes.
Frothy milk from four buffaloes sweetened with sugar.

And also pseudo curses like:

May they who scolded my little babu burn without food! May they waste away like red mud in water!

Through whatever was said or sung by whoever was at home or whoever was visiting, the language of the inner rooms entered my ears and spread out within me, without me being quite aware of what it meant. Isn't it primarily through the language of our inner rooms that we are initiated to a language and a culture that shapes our mind-set even when we do not yet know the name of that language? At the base of a language is the mother. Our minds are formed on her lap through her songs, her nurturing care, her stories. I must also mention a word from the world of women, from *streeloka*, a word I used to hear from my mother, *hadha*, balance. Bringing about a balance. This balance was not something which could be measured, not something clearly defined. Each person had to find the appropriate balance. This concept of balance we have in India is to be found more in our kitchens and the inner life of our homes than in the lives of sages. My desire is to achieve in my writing, the balance I have heard about in the inner world of the home.

My mother used to sing a long song while patting babies to sleep. It was the story of Anasuya, and the Divine Trinity, Brahma, Vishnu, and Maheshwara. The Trinity come as suggested by their wives to test the chastity of Anasuya, the ascetic wife of sage Athri. They ask her to feed them without wearing any clothes. She is not unnerved by the divine request. Through the power of her penance, Anasuya transforms them into babies and nurses them in the nude. From one of the inner rooms, Mother's lullaby would softly waft out in waves to our ears while we were playing, studying, ... We used to enter the story by cheering the quick-witted Anasuya who could change the Trinity into babies and teach Saraswathi, Lakshmi, and Parvathi a lesson in humility.

And now? The same story from the Puranas[1] has become the universal theme of any woman's ability to deftly overcome any predicament with her sense of self-worth. The way Anasuya passed the test with her dignity intact has come down to us in songs and stories through our language; first by word of mouth, *moukhika*, and later, in books. Many such stories have shaped our mind-set long before we were aware of our identity as Indians. This is how the world-view of a people is nurtured, from budding on the mother's lap to blossoming in the world outside. This is why we see language as mother. Language becomes the goddess of the people; literature becomes their wealth, their Bhuvaneshwari, the Goddess of the Earth. And this Bhuvaneshwari becomes a blessing to the world.

In this translation of *Asprushyaru* into English as *Vasudeva's Family*, I see my novel moving out of the inner rooms to the world beyond, transcending language and cultural barriers.

[1] Puranas: myths and legends. Here, the same old stories.

Susheela and I spent three days reading the novel together and enjoying the flow of the story from one language to the other. While reading her version, I felt I was reading the story in Kannada. I thank Mini Krishnan for getting *Asprushyaru* translated into English by Susheela Punitha and for the zeal with which she led us through the process as if it were a mission. I thank Tejaswini Niranjana for her translation of my 'writer's pages' that provides the context for my writing and K.S. Vaishali for the detailed introduction that gives an idea of Modern Kannada Literature.

Manipal, 2012   Vaidehi

Translator's Note

While translating the title, *Asprushyaru*, I grew in leaps and bounds as a translator, stretching my idea of negotiating with the text of the novel beyond its theoretical boundaries in a bid to be true to its spirit, its intention.

A literal translation of the title into English would be *Untouchables*, bringing to mind Mulk Raj Anand's classic, *Untouchable*. The word connotes strongly with the depressed classes, the outcastes. But Vaidehi's novel is a different take on the problem, implicating intra-caste hierarchies as much as inter-caste politics based on touch and untouch. To the question, 'who is untouchable?' the book replies, 'everyone!' It questions personal attitudes, not merely social, and their bearing on personal aspirations, not only relationships.

But it also moves beyond the segregation that comes with differences between castes and classes to the connections we forge with one another because of the similarity in our experiences. So, the title, *Asprushyaru*, could not be translated; it had to be trans-created.

Here, the intention of the text helped. The head of the household, Vasudevaraya, tries to make the ideal *Vasudhaiva Kutumbakam* (*the whole earth is one family*) as real as possible in his home. In his compassion for Thukri who is with child, he brings her to his house to be tended during childbirth and after. The word for compassion in Hebrew, *rakham/racham*, refers to womb in the singular and in the plural extends to mean compassion, equivalent to an unconditional concern for the helpless. Vasudevaraya takes Thukri into his home, his family, his womb. But the title cannot, therefore, become *Vasudevaraya's Family* because the protagonist's name is Vasudeva. The *raya* is merely the suffix generally added to define Brahminical antecedents. Vasudeva, the person, steps out of his Brahminical confines to fulfil his basic human urge to be compassionate. And that is how the trans-created title became *Vasudeva's Family*, to hold the positive energies in the novel.

Most of the other problems arose out of the cultural differences between the author and me; though we are Kannadigas, we are from different parts of Karnataka. But they were easily sorted out in the few days I spent with her, reading the text to her in English to see if it carried the same sense and flavour as the regional dialect of Kannada she uses in the original. For instance, what better understanding of her version of *ganji* could I get than have her cook par-boiled rice almost a whole morning and serve it to me as gruel for lunch with all the other side-dishes her story talks about! My version of *ganji* is a porridge we make with ragi flour; it takes around ten minutes.

My special thanks to Mini Krishnan, my editor, for providing me with this opportunity to grow as a translator. I am indebted to her editorial input for she honed my skills by advising me to work the meanings of words into the context wherever possible to keep the footnotes to a minimum. She asked for extra sentences to ease the flow when the cultural transfer from a coastal town to a global readership became dense and she recast them wherever they became tortuous. She also suggested chapter-headings as sign-posts. With her able guidance, I could work with two languages to create a third tailor-made for *Vasudeva's Family*.

Mini has expanded the scope of the of the work by asking Tejaswini Niranjana for her translation of Vaidehi's autobiographical note which Tejaswini has very graciously made available.

Bangalore, 2012   Susheela Punitha

Introduction

Kannada Literary Heritage and Marginalized Voices

With a seamless and an unbroken literary history of fifteen hundred years, Kannada language and literature occupy a pre-eminent position among the literatures of the Indian sub-continent. The earliest example of a full-length Kannada language stone inscription containing Brahmi characters with graphological characteristics attributed to those of proto-Kannada in Old Kannada script can be found in the Halmidi stone inscription dated about AD 450.

Kannada literary history dates back to the reign of the kings of the Rashtrakuta dynasty and the emergence of the first seminal work in Kannada literary criticism entitled *Kavirajamarga* during the reign of King Nrupatunga of this dynasty in ninth century AD is hailed as an epoch making event in the annals of Kannada literary heritage.

Nevertheless, this literary history essentially has had a male supremacist orientation. Therefore, it is no small wonder that the marginalized voices in the pages of Kannada literature have been those of women. Women writers are unheard of in the corridors of the Kannada literary establishment. Though tracing the literary subculture of women writers and their writings from the annals of early Kannada literary history is indeed a daunting task, its importance can hardly be over-emphasized. Female literary creativity has always had to contend precariously with too many patriarchal surveillance mechanisms that thwart its expression. In the ancient pages of Kannada literature, Kanthi has the distinction of being the first woman poet. Eulogized and lauded as 'Abhinava Vagdevi' a veritable incarnation of the Goddess of learning, Kanthi is known to have been a contemporary of the poet Nagachandra of the eleventh century AD. Given the almost quasi-mythical status of Kanthi owing to insufficient historical evidence, the incipient female voices of creative articulation are those of the Kannada vachanakarthis in the context of twelfth century Kalyana and the 'Anubhava Mantapa', a philosophical forum established by Basavanna, the great social reformer renowned for his revolutionary zeal. Alongside the famous vachanakaras and principal saints of the Veerashiva movement in Karnataka like Allama Prabhu and Basavanna, there are the vachanakarthis like Akka Mahadevi, Aydakki Lakkamma, the wife of Aydakki Marayya, Kadira Remmavve, Sule Sankavva, Kalavve, the wife of Urilingapeddi who was a prominent vachanakara from the lower caste of Shudras, Dhoopada Goggavve, Basavanna's wife Neelambike, and others who have written tremendously insightful and unforgettable vachanas.

Sanchiya Honnamma (Seventeenth Century) and Thereafter

After the twelfth century vachanakarthis, there seems to be a long hiatus and an interregnum of over four centuries after which we hear of Sanchiya Honnamma in the seventeenth century. She was known as 'Sarasasahityada Varadevate' which literally meant the 'Goddess of exquisite poetry' (a title bestowed upon her by her mentor, the court poet Singaracharya). Honnamma, a talented poet and a conventional thinker who upheld the virtues of a 'pativrata shiromani' (a wife devoted to her husband was considered to be the ideal of womanhood) wrote 'Hadibadeya Dharma' (Duties of a Devoted Wife). Shringaramma, a contemporary of Honnamma, was the first poet among women to have composed a long wedding song 'Padmini Kalyana' in a prosody called 'sangatya', celebrating the legendary wedding of the celestial couple, Lord Ventakeshwara of Tirupathi, believed to be the incarnation of lord Vishnu and princess Padmavathi, the daughter of king Akasharaya, also known as the incarnation of Goddess Mahalakshmi, the divine consort of Lord Mahavishnu. Later, in the eighteenth century, queen Cheluvambe, the fourth queen of King Dodda Krishna Raja Wodeyar (1713–1732) of Mysore composed verses on the same theme entitled 'Venkatachala Mahatmya Lalipada' which was sung as a lullaby. Cheluvambe also composed a poetic work called 'Varanandi Kalyana' in 'sangatya' metre, containing 881 verses. This remarkable work is a creative synthesis of the various strands of mythopoeic imagination, quasi-historical sources, legends, and religious beliefs by the poet. It is a beautiful narration of the love of a Muslim princess from Delhi for Lord Cheluvarayaswamy of Melukote set in the time of Ramanujacharya, the Vaishnava saint who undertook the reconstruction of Cheluvanarayanaswamy temple in Melukote.

Haridasa Parampara and Women Poets

The Vaishanava saints of Karnataka enriched the Kannada literary canon through innumerable 'Haridasa keertane', verses composed in praise of Lord Vishnu. The contributions of saints like Purandaradasa, Kanakadasa, Vijaya Vittala Dasa, and others to the classical music and literary traditions of Karnataka were noteworthy. They also enriched the socio-cultural imaginary of their times and undoubtedly have great contemporary relevance as well. But what goes unnoticed is the significant contributions of women poets to this 'Haridasa Parampara'. Poets like Galagali Avva, her disciple Bhagamma, saint Helavanakatte Giriyamma, Harapanahalli Bhimavva, Yadugiriyamma, Shantibai, Orabai Lakshmidevamma, Ganapakka, Sundarabai, Bellary Radhabai, and others have written exquisite and flowing spiritual poetry enclosing 'madhura bhakti rasa' that also lends itself to outstanding musical form. These are some of the supreme instances of mellifluous versification by women who quietly led their lives around the fringes of this great literary movement which was also a unique socio-religious movement in Karnataka.

The Modern Kannada Novel and Women Novelists

The salient phases of modern Kannada literature—Navodaya, Pragatisheela, Navya, Navyottara, and Bandaya have produced several noteworthy women poets, novelists, and short story writers.

Nanjanagudu Tirumalamba (1887–1982) can be considered as the forerunner of the modern Kannada women novelists although another woman writer, Shanthabai Nilagara, had written a novel called *Sadguni Krishnabai* as early as in 1908 before the publication of Tirumalamba's first novel *Susheela*. Tirumalamba was a woman of exceptional courage and grit. Born in 1887, in Nanjanagudu of the old Mysore province, Tirumalamba was able to receive primary school education due to the encouragement of her father Venkatakrishna Iyengar. Born into a traditional Brahmin family, Tirumalamba was married off to Narasimha Iyengar of Kollegala at the tender age of ten and four years later she lost her husband and led the life of a traditional Hindu Brahmin widow for the rest of her long life. She was educated by her father at home, reading the Ramayana and the Mahabharata and various Kannada texts. She was not given any kind of formal education. Altogether, Tirumalamba wrote twenty-eight books between 1908 and 1939, her most important works were published between 1908 and 1915. The main reason for this was that in 1913, she established a printing press and published all her novels herself. Her other literary works were *Nabha*, *Vidyullata*, *Viragini*, *Dashakanya*, *Ramananda*, *Vikarama*, *Chandravadana*, *Purnakanta*, *Bhadra Geetvali*, *Nishakanta*, etc.

Although Tirumalamba was a prolific writer and her versatility was revealed in her works which ranged from a Yakshagana to drama, from prose essays to short stories, autobiography and also poetry, it was obvious that the novel was her principal literary medium. She also edited two journals called *Matrunandini* and *Satihitaishini*. In 1939, Tirumalamba published her last novel *Manimala*. Her books were widely read in those days. As many as 2000 to 3000 copies of some of her books were sold and some novels were even reprinted thrice. These facts conclusively established her popularity. But Tirumalamba faded into oblivion and lost her readership when Shivarama Karanth, Masti Venkatesh Iyengar, and K.V. Puttappa began to write novels.

Saraswathibai Rajawade (1913–1994) who wrote as 'Giribale' was a prominent Kannada writer of the Navodaya phase. During the 1950s, Rajawade's articles appeared in all the newspapers and periodicals of Karnataka. Known to be very beautiful, Saraswathibai Rajawade had also acted in films before marrying Raya Shastri Rajawade, a great scholar based in Singapore. In spite of the restrictions imposed on her movements after marriage, Saraswathibai started writing for Kannada periodicals of those times such as *Tayinadu, Kantirava, Usha, Suvasini, Antaranga, Subhoda*, etc. Giribale's columns regularly appeared in the periodical 'Kathavali' for seven years. She was known for her progressive views and had sharply criticised the corrupt practices of Matadhipathis (religious pontiffs of Hindu mathas) so unhesitantly that it had greatly appealed to the 'dharmadhikari' of a pilgrimage centre. The great novelist Aa. Na. Krishnarao had openly expressed his admiration for her intrepidity.

Another talented poet whose precious works of poetry remained virtually unknown was Belagere Janakamma (1912–1948). Her literary talents were recognized by great writers like Da. Ra. Bendre and Masti Venkatesha Iyengar. Her poems were published in newspapers like *Jaya Karnataka* and *Prabudhha Karnataka*. Her poems dealt with a wife's hardships in the husband's house, ordeals of repeated pregnancies and childbirths and registered a feminist sensibility; although at times we see a note of anticlimax, abruptly surrendering to traditional virtues of wifely subordination. 'Did you think a woman's body was a plant that could go on yielding fruit endlessly?' Janakamma asks God in one of her poems in anguish. She died at 36 in childbirth but had managed to write more than a hundred poems and had published a poetry collection entitled *Kalyana*. Writer Nemichandra who has passionately written about the achievements of women writers of the past like Shyamala Devi, Kalyanamma, Savitramma, and others has also written about Belagere Janakamma who despite just two years of schooling had written some remarkable poems during the pre-Independence era.

The literary achievements of the young widow R. Kalyanamma (1891–1965) and her work for education and rehabilitation of poor women were commendable. The founder of Shri Sharada Sthri Samaja in 1913 and Makkala Koota in 1938 in Bangalore, Kalyanamma created a forum for women to learn languages, attend lectures, and participate in discussions. She expressed her views in leading newspapers like *Sadhvi, Kodagu, Nudigannadi, Vidyadayini*, etc. Kalyanamma also wrote several novels during her lifetime.

H.V. Savitramma (1913–1992) is another prominent writer in the senior generation of Kannada women novelists. Savitramma published her first work in 1949 and continued writing till 1990. Even during those times when education for women had not gained any importance in Indian society, Savitramma graduated with three gold medals. She expressed her progressive views on women's emancipation in her novels and short stories. Proficient in English and Hindi, Savitramma translated the novels of Tagore such as *Gora* and *Ghare Baire* and Russian writer Anton Chekov's short stories. Her novel *Seethe-Rama-Ravana* is a feminist revisioning of the epic. One of the famous exponents of 'Navya' school, contemporary writer Nemichandra, in praise of Savitramma's revisionist attempts, remarks, 'It is interesting that even at an early time some women writers like Savitramma have tried to interpret our epics from the female character's point of view.'

M.K. Indira, Triveni, and Anupama Niranjana are the major women novelists of the Pragatisheela phase of modern Kannada literature. Unlike H.V. Savitramma, M.K. Indira (1917–1994) could not even complete her primary school education, yet she went on to write forty-eight novels. Indira started writing at the age of 45 and her first novel *Tunga Bhadra* was published in 1963. The idealism of the Navodaya writers was abundantly present in her novels but her works also had a woman-centred outlook. Indira in her novels like *Gejje Puje (First Performance)*, *Phaniyamma*, and *Sadananda* explored the issues of prostitution, child marriage, female subjugation, illiteracy of women, exploitation of widows, widow remarriage, etc.

Although there are many other Kannada women novelists belonging to the earlier phases of the evolution of the Kannada novel of the earlier decades of twentieth century, the salient contributions of novelists like Anasuya Shankar (Triveni), Anupama Niranjana, and Veena Shanteshwara to the modern Kannada novel can hardly be over-emphasized. They are very important links in the female literary tradition of the modern Kannada novel and their works constitute another milestone in the history and evolution of feminist consciousness in the modern and contemporary Kannada novel. Women writers from minority communities like Muslim writer Sara Aboobaker in her novel *Chandragiriya Tiradalli* (on the Banks of the river Chandragiri, in 1982) have raised sensitive questions about the rights of Muslim women and their oppressive realities. She depicted the unenviable life of Muslim women due to practices like the triple 'talaq' prevalent among the Muslims. She was the first Kannada writer to throw light on the life of Muslim women within the four walls of their houses and their suppressed existence behind the purdah. Sara began her career as a writer when the women's movement gathered momentum in India with the celebration of the International Year of Women in 1975.

Anasuya Shankar (1928–1963) known by her pseudonym 'Triveni' became an extremely popular novelist during her lifetime and wrote twenty novels in the span of a decade. Triveni's works were regarded as intensely feminist in their content and depicted the psychological problems faced by middle-class Indian women. She wrote about problems like hysteria and puerperal psychosis in women in her novel *Sharapanjara* (A Cage of Arrows) in 1965. Her other novels are *Modala Hejje* (The First Step) in 1956, *Sotu Geddavalu* (Defeated, She Won) in 1956, *Keelugombe* (The Mechanical Doll) in 1958, *Durada Betta* (The Distant Hill) in 1962, and *Bekkina Kannu* (The Cat's Eye) in 1964.

Anupama Niranjana (1934–1991) was a doctor by profession who wrote twenty major novels, eight collections of short stories, and several medical books on women's health. Her novel *Madhavi* (1976) was a feminist reconstruction of the tale of King Yayati's daughter Madhavi based on an episode from the Mahabharata. In her feminist recasting of the mythical story of Madhavi, Anupama Niranjana raises sharp questions about the sexual objectification of women and the notion of woman as an extension of man's property.

We can locate two central concerns in Veena Shanteshwara's (1945) fiction. If one is centred around self-exploration, the other revolves around liberation. Veena identifies a very important change in the contemporary woman's sensibilities. Many of her stories have shocked the average reader and shaken their attitudes about status quo. Veena Shanteshwara is one of the chief representatives of the new wave of women's writing started by Rajalakshmi Rao who explored the inner life of women in her collection of short stories *Sangama* (Confluence) and has identified herself with the feminist movement. Her short story collections of stories, *Mullugalu* (Thorns, 1968), *Koneya Dari* (The Last

Day, 1972), *Kavalu* (Cross-roads, 1976), and her novel *Gandasaru* (Men, 1975) depict the exploitation of women with a rare sensitivity and candour. She is one of the major women writers in the 'Navya' phase of the modern Kannada novel.

Prathibha Nandakumar, Vaidehi, Sara Aboobaker, Nagaveni, Savita Nagabhushana, and others are some of the prominent women writers of the post-Navya phase of modern Kannada literature. The literary works of Nagaveni, M.S. Veda, and Muslim writers like Sara Aboobaker have enriched 'Bandaya Sahitya' in Kannada. Nagaveni's *Gandhi Banda* (Gandhi Arrives) published in 1999 looks at an entire gamut of cultural and social experiences of various castes and classes against the backdrop of the Gandhian ideologies of the Indian independence movement. M.S. Veda's short stories delineate the predicaments of Dalits with a rare sensitivity using the rural dialects of T. Narsipura, Chamarajanagar, and Talkadu regions of Mysore district.

Alluding to the feminist spirit that pervades much of her writing, Nemichandra, the writer of collections of short stories like *Ondu Kanasina Sanje* says, 'To me, feminism is a part of humanism and a way of life. It is something I believed in much before I became aware of the term or the movement. Things have changed for the better but the world continues to be predominantly male-centric.'

Modern Kannada women novelists have handled the challenges of writing with an admirable sense of maturity and equanimity. They have grappled with the women's question in the context of modern and contemporary Kannada literature in fascinating ways. Many women writers, in their recasting of the stereotyped mythological, religious, and cultural representations of women, have shown how mainstream literature has functioned as a cultural weapon of male hegemony and perpetuated gender discriminatory practices in the name of universality, objectivity, and neutrality. Confronting the sexism and misogyny in literary, cultural, and social ideologies resourcefully, the novels of some of the contemporary Kannada women writers read against the grain of such 'sexual/textual politics'.

From the twentieth century, it is possible to think of the continuity of a female literary tradition in Kannada literature. In twentieth century's

Karnataka, we see an efflorescence of literary creation by Kannada women writers who gave Kannada literature an unmistakable edge. They are able to sensitively portray a world that has in it women rich in substance. They jerk the average Indian readers out of their typical Indian notions about gender issues. Women writers in Kannada have grappled with complex ideas such as sensuality, subjugation, and social discrimination. They have tried to evolve new critical paradigms to sensitise Kannada readership to the issues of gender politics, misogynistic representations of women in literary texts and the self-censorship exercised by women writers that frequently curb their sense of agency and creativity, camouflaging more disturbing questions of inequality. One of the prominent Kannada writers, Shailaja Uduchana, remarks, 'We of the older generation of writers have been wearing the veil of censorship like a nine yard saree'. For another writer Du. Saraswathi, 'What is interesting is the censorship within us, the cultural policeman who is inside us'.

Vaidehi: Life and Works

Vaidehi, who has been acclaimed as one of the most prominent and unique literary figures of contemporary India, began her literary career in the 1970s. Her metamorphosis from Janaki Hebbar and later Janaki Srinivas Murthy into Vaidehi is a fascinating one. A young and reticent Vaidehi had contributed an article called 'Neereyara Dina' (Women's Day) to the Kannada magazine *Sudha* and later requested them not to print the article as it contained many sensitive autobiographical details. Well, it was published nevertheless but there was also an ingenious solution for her predicament. That was the pseudonym 'Vaidehi'. Thus, Janaki came to be known as 'Vaidehi' in the Kannada literary world. Praising Vaidehi's creative genius, Lankesh, one of Karnataka's foremost writers says: 'It is difficult to appreciate contemporary writers. There may be a genuine camaraderie and empathic understanding between myself and other writers. But more than that, there will be a spirit of competition or rivalry. Sometimes, it may degenerate into the level of jealousy. Nevertheless, when I see genuinely talented writers who are my contemporaries, I am filled with a sense of wonder and they provide me refreshingly new insights and enhance my pride in authorship. They enrich me and greatly contribute to a sense of pride that I derive from my identity as an author: Vaidehi is one amongst such writers.'

Born in Kundapura, a small town in Udupi district of Karnataka, Vaidehi grew up in a large traditional Kannada Brahmin family with many siblings. Her father, Sri A.V.N. Hebbar, was a busy lawyer and Vaidehi's mother Mahalakshmamma was his second wife. In a large family, there was no time for the elders to supervise the children's studies and the children bonded with their siblings, cousins, relatives, servants, and neighbours. Thus, this was a microcosm. This world of her childhood reappears frequently in her fictional works. Vaidehi has a prolific literary output in Kannada. Her first short story collection 'Mara, Gida, Balli' (Tree, Bush, and Creeper) was published in 1979. Subsequently, the works published were *Antarangada Putagalu* (Pages from Within, 1984), 'Gola' (Globe, 1986), *Asprushyaru* the award winning novel (1982)—a collection of poetry *Bindu Bindige* (Drop Pot/Droplet, 1990), *Samajashastrajneya Tippanige* (1991), *Ammacchiyemba Nenapu* (2000), and *Krauncha Pakshikagalu* (2005). A collection of all the short stories published in 1979–2004 by Vaidehi entitled *Alegalalli Antaranga* has been published by Akshara Prakashana, Heggodu, in 2006. Writing about her first collection of short stories, K.V. Subbanna remarks that the fourteen short stories written over several years in the collection *Mara, Gida, Balli* record the evolution of a writer of integrity who writes in an unhurried manner. Vaidehi never sacrifices herself at the altar of literary craftsmanship in order to reconstruct her stories ingeniously. According to K.V. Subbanna, Vaidehi presents fascinating vignettes of life from her own experiences without any hesitation or misgivings. Invoking a musical metaphor, K.V. Subbanna comments that Vaidehi's stories are set in the 'Mandra sruti' (musical notes in the lower pitch of 'Saptaka'—a cluster of seven musical notes in music) and they silently captivate the readers like the caressive appeal of the musical notes from the lower pitch.

Vaidehi has translated two important feminist books from English into Kannada: Kamaladevi Chattopadhyay's *Indian Women's Struggle for Freedom* into Kannada as *Bharatiya Mahileyara Swatantra* in 1983 and Maitrayee Mukhopadhyay's *Silver Shackles* as '*Belliya Sankolegalu*' in 1985. Listening to the speeches of eminent music director and musicologist Bhasker

Chandavarker at his music appreciation workshops, Vaidehi taped his speeches and transcribed them into a script, translated it into Kannada, and brought out a precious volume of two hundred pages entitled '*Sangeeta Samvada*' in 1999. Perhaps a work of this unique depth cannot be found in any other Indian language. Her compilation of the memoirs of the writer Sediyapu Krishna Bhatta in *Sediyapu Nenapugalu* (1996) and well-known theatre personality B.V. Karanth entitled *Illiralare Allige Hogalare* (2003), besides her biography of the woman writer Smt Saraswati Bai Rajwade entitled *Muntada Kelaru Putagalu* (2008), are some of the finest examples of her limpid prose style. Her collection of prose writings, *Mallinatha Dhyana*, has emerged from her columns in *Lankesh Patrike*. Mallinatha is one of the Jain Thirthankaras (canonized saints). In some versions of followers of the Shwethambara sect of Jainism, Mallinatha is held to be the only Jain saint who attained salvation despite his effeminacy. The acolytes of the Digambara sect rule out salvation for women and have other narratives about this Thirthankara. But for Vaidehi, it is only in the meditative state of trance that Mallinatha realizes that an individual can transcend the irreconcilable polarities of masculinity and femininity and access a state of mind that goes beyond the male-female binary and the consequent reification of gender identities. Breaking free of the shackles of the mind, careening between the masculine and the feminine, perennially hemmed in by a sense of finitude yet hankering after a glimpse of liberation, it is a deepening state of immersion and philosophical reflection—perhaps this is what Vaidehi means by 'Mallinatha dhyana'. It is not an exaggeration to say that such a contemplative consciousness pervades Vaidehi's writings.

In her poetry collection *Bindu-Bindige*, Vaidehi interweaves the traditional songs sung by women in Kannada households with new insights and recasts myths in fascinating ways. This juxtaposition of the mythical and the traditional with the contemporary, transmitted through the woman's point of view, is a salient feature of this collection. Her poems alternate between the tender and the meditative with a remarkable sense of ease and fluidity. The poem 'Shivana meesuva hadu' (bathing Shiva) communicates Gowaramma's yearning for conjugal love and companionship which elude her as she has to compromise with a rather disloyal, philandering husband. Vaidehi forges a feminist poetics in her narration with exemplary linguistic ingenuity.

Vaidehi grew up registering the myriad details of the traditional orthodoxy-bound life around her, acquiring the basic nutrients which would enrich her creative writing. With rare sensitivity, she reconstructs them in her numerous short stories. Vaidehi also uses the Kundapura dialect in her fiction. Her stories are deeply rooted in this community and its cultural ethos. Naturally, the characters who hail from this community speak in this dialect. In many of her short stories, the characters are inseparable from the dialect in which they speak. Language bequeaths us many social voices and these voices construct both selves and characters as selves. Vaidehi uses these voices with remarkable aplomb. Vaidehi's stories leave an indelible imprint on our minds with their rich variety in linguistic experimentation and narrative strategies compatible with each story. Vaidehi also shows how the cultural context operates in order to fashion the self according to gender differences. Although so authentically local, these vignettes and reflections on woman's position, predicaments and potentialities, socio-cultural trends and values of human life acquire an extraordinary, unusual kind of universality. That is the literary achievement of Vaidehi. In an intimate, conversational, colloquial idiom, Vaidehi's stories explore the profoundest depths of life. It is a tribute paid to those small voices, often unheard, neglected, and ignored. Vaidehi gives a voice to the silent anguish and the helpless speechlessness of the gendered subaltern in her stories. Her powerful portrayals are born out of her interactions with many lower-caste domestics who worked in her household and in the neighbourhood where she grew up.

Vaidehi's fictional world revolves around women of different castes, age groups, and social strata. They also have different kinds of sensibilities and views on life. From the very traditional to the modern and liberated, from the unmarried to the widowed, from a home-maker to the sex worker all are covered in the expanse of her fictional world. Here, there are the educated as well as the unlettered, there are also thieves, lunatics, oppressors, and the oppressed and the dispossessed. In Vaidehi's stories, the women do not appear in a stereotypical mould. She challenges the practice of monolithic representations. This variety, this polyphony, and these protean possibilities have made Vaidehi one of our prominent writers; because life itself is polychromatic, reflecting myriad shades and colours. In her subtle and insightful portrayals, what is also clearly discernible is the profound wisdom that comprehends the many pressures which are operative in a given human situation. For Vaidehi, 'Writing is like *kasuti*—an embroidery of memories through which women try to forget their pain and understand their lives.' True, it is the woman's view point but there are no oversimplifications. It is not a facile kind of unproblematically univocal feminist or anti-men point of view. Vaidehi tackles questions of gender inequality with exemplary maturity. She is aware that gendering is the biggest institution in the world. Sexual difference is the only empirical difference, a tangible, palpable difference that is a perceivable reality. But it can never be a single monolithic issue for Vaidehi. Though a feminist consciousness is something that pervades her works over the decades, Vaidehi's writing is too complex to be accommodated within a single 'ism'.

Asprushyaru

In her novel *Asprushyaru* (1992), Vaidehi powerfully portrays how caste functions as a form of identification and exploitation and as a structure of disenfranchisement. Women cannot be represented as unmarked and disembodied from their caste and religious identity. She also connects issues of caste hierarchies with those of gender inequality by not examining them in isolation but emphasizing their shared and entangled histories.

Asprushyaru was a prize winning novel in the Yugadi competition for the best Kannada novel conducted by the Kannada magazine *Sudha* in 1982. A cursory glance at the title would suggest that perhaps the novel depicts the conditions of untouchables and focuses on the eradication of oppressive systems of discriminatory practices perpetuating untouchability. But Vaidehi's delineation of the caste consciousness in this novel is more complex and steers clear of any oversimplifications. Vaidehi shows how social stratification and hierarchization of communities on the basis of caste produce various forms of subjugation and vulnerability.

Vaidehi explores the notion of untouchability at multiple levels in this novel. One is at the level of a social hierarchy in the patterns of dominance and subordination visible in the relationships between Brahmins and Koragas. The other level refers to certain discriminatory practices among the Brahmins who consider themselves to be the most superior caste in the social hierarchy, where the Brahmin women are held to be unclean and impure at the time of menstruation, childbirth, etc., and therefore treated as untouchables. The irony is unmistakable when these Brahmin women who are considered to be impure during certain phases of their lives, treat the men and women of the lower castes like Koragas and other Shudra communities as untouchables. Vaidehi perceives the debilitating codes of conduct that discipline upper caste women and at the same time she also takes cognizance of their condescension towards women of the lower castes. The novel also highlights the triple forms of subjugation that lower caste women suffer at the hands of upper caste men and women. Lower caste women's vulnerability to sexual violence and harassment is well known. Their stigmatization by upper caste women and the economic exploitation of their labour are the other harsh realities they have to contend with besides their subjugation by lower caste men. Vaidehi also touches upon yet another subtle dimension of untouchability when Saroja, the younger sister of Rathna, who is repulsed by the insensitivity of her brother-in-law wonders if she like her sister Rathna would also end up marrying a man who may never reciprocate her feelings, who may never touch her heart and if she would also have insensitive children as products of such a soulless union.

Asprushyaru unveils the macabre and inhuman side of untouchability in certain episodes that profoundly disturb the reader. After the naming ceremony of Rathna's baby, when the untouchable woman Narpate and her people feast on the leftovers chasing away the crows and dogs and the circumstances that lead to the tragic death of the Koosa woman in childbirth due to haemorrhage, neglect, apathy, and indifference of the hospital staff chillingly portray the inhumanity of the system. Vaidehi also draws our attention to the ways in which caste ideologies draw on biological metaphors of defilement to enable differentiated conceptions of personhood. In this way, caste becomes a form of embodiment, marking the human body as pure or impure. Criticizing the ideological fabric of Hindu patriarchy in her essay 'Stri-Purush Tulana' (1882) which is perhaps the first full-fledged feminist critique in the context of the history of Indian feminism, Marathi writer Tarabai Shinde denounces the caste hierarchies that disempower the lower caste woman and the upper caste widow. Vaidehi raises these issues in *Asprushyaru*. She illustrates how austere widowhood becomes a powerful symbol of upper caste patriarchy. The enforcement of widowhood shows how caste morality is regulated through gender. There is also a very insightful and perceptive critique of the Brahminical ideology which works in ingenious ways to create a complex structure of hierarchy where the lower castes themselves are graded into less polluting and more polluting castes with the former exercising power over the latter.

Vaidehi and Feminist Discourse

There are no theoretical discourses on feminism in Vaidehi's writings but this feminist consciousness unfolds as a part of life itself and it is so inseparably intertwined with life. 'I am angry when they use words like a "woman writer", a "woman centred work", etc. Because no one refers to anyone as a "male writer" or talks about a "male centred theme". We talk only about human beings and that human being happens to be a woman. What is the meaning of mainstream literature? Then, how should we make sense of those tributaries and sub-streams? If you are going to disregard women, then what kind of a mainstream ideology would that be?' retorts Vaidehi. This is her unequivocal stance towards the issue of gender politics within the institution of literature. From her first collection of short stories *Mara, Gida, Balli* to *Krauncha Pakshikagalu* which is her latest collection of short stories, Vaidehi has written more than a hundred short stories. Although she never wavers from her allegiance to the portrayal of women's experiences in her writings, she does not succumb to melodrama. Her stories radiate a mature outlook where sarcasm, rage, cynicism, and rebellious feelings do not occupy the topmost layers but sink into the subliminal levels acquiring interlinear kinds of subtle undertones. Her works have had a wider reach through translations. Vaidehi's stories and poems have appeared in English translation in anthologies such as *The Inner Courtyard* edited by Lakshmi Holmström, *Women's Writing in India: 600 BC to the Present* edited by Susie Tharu and K. Lalita, *Gulabi Talkies and Other Stories—English Translations of 20 Stories* edited by Tejaswini Niranjana, *Jathre—The Temple Fair* translated by Nayana Kashyap and edited by Mini Krishnan, *From*

Kaveri to Godavari edited by Ramachandra Sharma, *The Southern Harvest* edited by Gita Hariharan, and *In their Own Voice: The Penguin Anthology of Contemporary Indian Women Poets* edited by Arlene R.K. Zide. Her stories have been translated into other Indian languages like Marathi, Malayalam, Telugu, Tamil, and Hindi. Vaidehi's literary works have rightly earned her a recognition as one of India's foremost writers.

Bangalore, 2012 K.S. Vaishali

Kinship Terms

appa, appayya	father (ayya—suffix denoting respect for a man)
anna, annayya	elder brother
akka	elder sister
maga, magu (plural: makkale)	child
mani, babanna	boy
henne, hudugi	girl
putti, babu, ammu, ammi, mari	baby
maharaya	young man, a variation of 'maharaja'
maharayithi	young lady, a variation of 'maharani'
ajja	grandfather
ajji	grandmother, old lady
bhavayya	elder brother-in-law
athigay	elder sister-in-law
mavaiyya	mother's brother, father's sister's husband, father-in-law (also, a term of respect for an elderly man and a humorous reference to prison being one's father-in-law's house, providing free food)

athe	mother-in-law, father's sister, mother's brother's wife (also, a term of respect for an elderly lady)
sosay	daughter-in-law
odeya, odeyare (plural used for respect too)	master
odathi	mistress
sannayya, channodeya (sanna, channa=little, odeya=master)	little master
channamma, channodathi	little mistress

one

A Birth

As soon as she came home from school, Shami ran to the midwife's house on Church Road.

'Akka has started a stomach ache. Amma wants you to come and see her.'

The midwife was combing Irene's hair. Irene was Shami's classmate. She wore socks and shoes to school, and pretty dresses too. But she was as stupid as stupid can be and did not even know what three times three was.

'Come! Come in!' said the midwife. And to Shami's message, she replied haltingly, 'O that means you'll soon have a son to play with.' Not that she could not speak Kannada fluently; she spoke it as Konkani Christians do, pronouncing every syllable distinctly.

'Si! A son?' grimaced Shami.

'Aha, why such disgust? One day you'll have a son of your own, anyway. What'll you say then?'

And turning to a girl folding clothes, 'Mary, get a glass of milk and some bread for Shyamala.'

Abbabba! Hadn't Parthakka warned her: 'Don't eat anything in her house! Those people eat meat. Tell her what your mother said and run back home.' And so Shami shouted, 'I don't want anything. I'm going!' and she raced back as fast as she had reached there.

'Amma, I too want a bob-cut like Irene,' cried Shami, trying to throw a tantrum as soon as she reached home.

'And what else?' asked Gowramma, carrying on with whatever she was doing, 'You sing a new tune every day, anyway.'

'Whenever I see you, you're working. I wish the midbai[1] was my mother,' grumbled Shami, loud enough for her mother to hear her. But when she came with a stick in hand, shouting, 'Say that again!' where was Shami? She was up in the attic by the little window, making faces.

'Won't you ever come down? Then, I'll peel the skin off your back.'

When Shami did come down after quite some time, Gowramma was talking to the midwife. Though she came and sat next to her mother, Shami took care not to sit too close. Hadn't she said she would peel the skin off her back? But her mother did not even notice her; she was too preoccupied.

In the next room, Rathna paced up and down labouriously as if she was obeying orders.

'Let's watch,' said the midwife as she was leaving, 'It doesn't look like she'll have the baby in a hurry. She may take time. Send word as soon as the pains get stronger. I'll come at once.'

Shami had wanted to eat the bread so badly. 'Parthakka shouldn't have asked me not to eat in her house. So what if they eat meat? Would the bread have eaten meat? By the way, how do they make bread, I wonder? When I go there again, I must eat it.'

Rathna stopped pacing and sat on the bed. Gowramma's eyes filled to see her daughter's face withered like a bunch of greens.

'If *you* shed tears in front of her ...' said Parthakka gruffly as she came into the room, and turning to Rathna, 'Here, drink this jeerige kashaaya,[2] maga. It's the best medicine. If the pain is due to gas, it'll go away but if it is labour pains, it'll come on stronger.' Rathna drank the herbal brew. The door was ajar and Shami was peeping in.

'Can't you send her out?' Rathna said. It did not sound like her voice at all; it was that weak.

---

[1] midbai: midwife

[2] jeerige kashaaya: brew of cumin seeds

Gowramma laughed. 'That girl wants to know everything. Do you know what she asked me yesterday? She wanted to know how babies come out. "By slitting open the stomach," I said. That's when she shouted, "I won't ever have a baby".' Rathna too laughed, gripping the bedpost and clenching her teeth.

Parthakka added her bit. 'That's what you have to tell her. That girl wants to know everything about everyone. Wait, the midbai will come now with a knife. If you hang around here, she might cut open your belly and hand you a baby.'

'She'll cut open *your* tummy,' Shami shot back, but she did not stand there. She ran out to where Putta and Jaya were playing. She had an announcement to make, hadn't she? 'Rathnakka has a stomach ache. In a little while the baby will be born!'

Saroja had served the children an early dinner. Putta and Jaya were nodding off by bedtime. The baby was not born yet, only assurances came from the birthing room: 'now' ... 'in just a while'. Saroja's eyelids grew heavy. She was tired as she had to see to everything in the house and look after Rathna's elder son, Ravi, as well. 'Mani, call me as soon as the baby comes,' she called out to Shiva, 'Ravi's sleepy. I'm getting him to bed.'

'Hm, mm,' said Shiva, 'The child's just an excuse. Sarojakka's sleepy.'

Now, only Shiva and Shami kept vigil.

Time ticked away.

When Gowramma came out and said, 'Can't you go to bed, children?' they said, 'Hm,' but did not stir.

'Ei, Shiva, how're babies born?' Shami asked her elder brother in a whisper.

'Don't you have anything better to talk about? Sit quietly.' Shiva looked at her with a sense of importance. Not to betray his ignorance, he made a face as if he knew but would not tell her.

'They cut open the stomach, they said,' Shami spoke in his ear.

'That's what they should do to someone like you.'

'Shut up!'

'Shami, will you stitch up your lips for a while? Why're you sitting up anyway, missing sleep, at this time of the night?' Gowramma shouted from the room.

They could hear the midwife, 'There ... there ... slo...o...w...ly. Just one more push.'

'Then? If you want babies, do they happen easily?' This from Parthakka.

'Children, go to bed.' Gowramma called out again.

Neither of them got up. Shami moved over and sat closer to Shiva.

'You know, the other day when the buffalo had a calf? The kasa[3] did not fall out the whole night. Seethu sat with a lantern waiting for it to come out. I believe the buffalo will not give milk if it eats it. I sat with her however much Amma asked me to go and sleep ... Abba! What a stink of fish from her!'

'What else? Will there be any other smell from fish-eaters?'

'You know what kind of stories she told me that night? She said there's a haiguli-daiva[4] beyond the backyard. That demon will not allow the kasa to fall quickly after a calf is born. But Seethu had already put a charm on the buffalo with some herbs. On Sunday, during the genda, she'll find out why Kempi isn't giving us milk. She said one day she'll take us to the genda to see her people walk on live coal. You can come if you want to.... At last the kasa fell. She put it in a pot, dug a pit and buried it.'

'What's kasa?'

Aha! Now it was Shami's turn to feel important. She had also asked Seethu the same question but she had not explained that it was the afterbirth; she had only replied, 'Kasa means kasa.' And so now, Shami also said, 'Kasa is kasa. Don't you know even that?'

'Your head!'

'*Your* head!'

'Won't you shut up, children? Why aren't you sleepy?'

'Ammaaaaaaaaaaaaaa!' screamed Rathna with all her might. After a while, there was a baby's cry. Shami sat up with a start, 'Magu!'

'Yes, it's surely a boy,' said Shiva.

'No! A girl!'

'Want to bet?'

---

[3] kasa: after-birth
[4] haiguli-daiva: demi-god

'Bet? Bet what?'

'If I win, I'll punch you.'

'And if I win, I'll ...'

'You won't win. Don't worry,' said Shiva.

Before Shami could start a fight Parthakka called out from the room, 'Maga, should I remind you to drop the harivaana?'[5]

'Che, it's a girl. I so much wanted to blow the conch,' said Shiva as he got up immediately and dropped the big brass plate with a clang.

Vasudevaraya, who had been waiting in the front verandah, came in and asked, 'Are the mother and child well?'

'Hm.'

'Did you check the time?'

'Hm. Twelve thirty-one. But the midbai says it was twelve thirty-five by her watch.'

'Our clock is correct.'

Vasudevaraya looked at the children. 'What is this? Children shouldn't miss their sleep.'

He had spoken just two sentences but they were worth their weight in gold.

'Hm,' said both of them and stood up. Before Shami could punch him with, 'Hey, I won! It's a girl. You said ...' Shiva said, 'What did Appayya say just now? I've got to go and sleep. If you open your mouth again, I'll tell Appayya.' As they went towards the bedroom, Gowramma mumbled, 'I told them so many times. Did they listen? And he told them just once. See how they walked with their tails crumpled? As they say, water becomes theertha only when it is dripped from the conch.'

'Thank God, the baby was born before the dark night of amavasya, even before Amavasye Boodhi . I'd made a vow to Aanegudde Ganapathi,' said Parthakka.

'I too,' joined Gowramma.

'Then Ganapathi will make a great profit,' said Shiva, going to Saroja and shaking her. 'Eii, Sarojakka, Sarojakka, Rathnakka has had her baby. A girl. Get up, ei! Then why did you ask me to wake you up? Can't you get up even if I shake you?'

---

[5] The conch is blown when a son is born.

Saroja did not wake up. She was always like that; she slept the sleep of the dead. Putta and Jaya were fast asleep too.

Shami tried to sleep but could not. She came to the door of the birthing room and called out to her mother, 'Amma, I want to see the baby.'

'Come in,' said Gowramma, opening the door a little.

'Don't let her in. She'll say, "Rathnakka ..." and may even come and sit beside her. What does *she* know about madi or mylige?'

'Then peep in from there, maga.'

Shami looked in from the door. Rathna was lying on a mattress on the floor. Towards the other wall, Parthakka was spreading a mat to sleep on. But she could not see the baby. She looked about a bit. Then she saw it; hands and feet wrapped in white cloth with only the face showing. A red face, red lips, closed eyes. Ooo, how cute! How like a baby sparrow ... a chick ... a darling!

'Amma, I want to carry the baby.'

'No, no, you can't touch her now. Let the bit of the cord fall off from the navel. Only then.'

'What's the cord from the navel?'

Gowramma did not scold her this time. 'I'll tell you tomorrow,' she said gently, 'Go and sleep now. I'll come in a while.'

'If only I were sleeping in Akka's place. The baby would've been beside me in the gerasi,'[6] thought Shami.

Parthakka sat down stretching her legs and grumbling about the midwife who might have reached home by now, 'However much I moved away from her, she'd move close enough to touch me, that woman with no care for earth or heaven.'

'Madi is just our practice, that's all. Anyway, aren't we also myligay now?' asked Gowramma.

'This defilement belongs to *our* house. The midwife's is the pollution of a hundred houses. She was saying she had delivered Sheshu Poojari's daughter's baby just before coming here. Didn't you hear that? Why should I become unclean with all the pollution from whomever *she* visits?' Parthakka argued.

[6] gerasi: winnowing fan made of cane

The new moon came round four days later. Narpate, the Koraga woman, came with every new moon.

'Isn't it Ammasi today, Amma?' she said, laughing. Her hair glistened with oil, the gift from every house she had visited, making you wonder if her head was a pot of oil. Sometimes she had a huge red dot of kumkuma[7] on her forehead, sometimes she did not. Her face and hands were tattooed. 'If we don't get tattooed here, after we die Yamadharma will pierce us with the tip of a snake's tail,' was her belief.

'Narpate's come! Narpate's come! Narpate! Narpate!' shouted Putta as he came running. Narpate laughed to see her channodeyaru, her darling little master. But then laughter came easily to her. She wore a cap of areca sheath and carried a cane basket in one hand. On her waist were five or six baskets, big ones or small, piled one on top of the other. Every once in a while, Gowramma bargained with her to buy a few, paying her with some rice or four annas. After they were bought, Chandu drew water from the well, poured it over them and only then did she bring them in. They were not to be touched until they were ritually purified.

Narpate had no husband. In fact she had nothing to call her own; she was an outcast. Whenever she was asked why she had not got married, she giggled. 'Her chest is flat. Who'll marry her?' said Chandu. Sometimes Chandu asked, 'Is she a man or a woman?' as if she cared, but it was only to provoke laughter. Whenever Narpate came, oil was poured into a coconut shell which was circled round each head. Some who seemed to have bad luck were made to look at the reflection of their faces in the oil and it was given to her. Then ill-luck fled from the family.

'It's because Narpate has been sucking in all our bad-luck that misfortune has soaked right through her,' Parthakka told the children.

As soon as she heard Putta shouting, 'Narpate!' Parthakka closed the window and door that were slightly ajar in the room where the new mother and her baby were. Nevertheless, Narpate stood outside. 'I heard the little Amma has had a baby ... I believe it's a girl ... then, Amma will sweeten our mouths with payasa,'[8] she said adding joy to joy.

---

[7] kumkuma: a dot of sanctified red powder that Hindus put between the eyebrows; a widow has to give up this auspicious practice.

[8] payasa: a sweet dish

'The baby's lovely,' said Putta.

'Yes, lovely, channodeyare,' repeated Narpate.

'She's red all over,' added Jaya.

'Yes, odathi, she's red all over,' she nodded. That was Narpate, always nodding, always echoing with a smile whatever anyone else said, with no sense of self-hood.

Parthakka called Putta and Jaya inside and scolded them, 'Don't say such things about the baby. You'll draw the evil eye on it, that's what's going to happen. Where's the need to be talking to such useless people and telling them everything, anyway? Gowreeee, can't you hurry up and give her the oil? Let her move on.'

'Is there a servant here to ready things and give it to her as soon as she arrives? Let her wait,' murmured Gowramma.

Jaya ran out again.

'Channamma,' said Narpate in a fondling voice.

'Ei, where d'you live?'

'I? ... oh, there ... beyond Naribena field.'

'Can I come? Just once?'

'Shhh ... it's not a place you can come to, odathi.'

'Go with her. We'll get you married to her son. With whoever comes, you start a tasteless chatter like cooking greens with no salt. Get right in,' Gowramma scolded Jaya as she brought the oil, placing it at a distance.

'Ayyo, don't scold her. She's just a child, Amma. So, when is the sweet coming?' When she did not get a reply, Narpate thought it was but natural, took the coconut-shell of oil and went on her way, trailing her tinkling laughter.

'Look at her, Amma,' said Chandu, who was sweeping the yard, 'This Narpate has a joy that no one else has. Am I wrong? One thing I've noticed; people who have nothing are always laughing. It's we who're weighed down all the time.'

Gowramma did not respond to her directly but said, 'Who does she think she is to say *we*? Does she think she's equal to *us*?' loud enough for Chandu to hear her, and she went indoors.

From that day the baby cried for four days, fusing days with nights. She could not put her lips to her mother's breasts to suck the milk squirting continuously; she was that spent with crying. She did not stop even though Parthakka had her on her lap the whole night and rained down songs on her. Rathna was exhausted with pain as her breasts became engorged. She had lumps in her armpits, her breasts felt hard and heavy. What could they do? Maadhu, the oil vendor, was upset to see Rathna suffering so much. 'Ayyo, Amma, you've had so many babies! Don't you know a charm for this? Lay a string of jasmines on each breast. The milk will flow out and the tightness will go away.' As soon as they got two strands of jasmines and laid them loosely on the breasts, the milk melted and flowed out easily like water, just as she had said.

'Ayyo! What a waste of milk! The baby could've drunk it,' grieved Rathna.

'Will the breasts make milk again?' worried Parthakka.

Parthakka's fears proved right. The breasts that were filled to bursting became soft and sagging once they lost their milk. Parthakka used all her wits to get them to make milk again. 'Grind jeerige and jaggery,[9] mix it in coconut milk, and give it to her every day,' said someone. Everyone had their own suggestions.

'It's like the proverb, the baby went back to the womb listening to the different things different people said,' laughed Parthakka. 'All this is because of that Narpate's eye. I can't even get rid of the evil; we're still mylige. If her eyes can have such an effect when she hasn't even seen the baby, what if she had!'

'Abah! I've had enough of babies. I'll ask him to get operated,' said Rathna.

'Will your husband get it done because you said so? He may do it only if *he* thinks he should,' said Gowramma, proud that her son-in-law had a mind of his own.

Parthakka did not like what Rathna said.

'What kind of bravado is this to say you don't want to have babies just because your baby cried? Are you a woman?'

'Do we have to be having babies just because we're women? What a story!' Saroja joined in the discussion.

'Yes, we have to. If my husband was alive, I would've had babies as long as I could.'

[9] jaggery: molasses

The children stopped eating their ganji[10] and burst out laughing. Even Parthakka, sitting in a corner, laughed. Gowramma too.

'I can't imagine Parthakka with a bulging tummy,' grimaced Shami.

'Why, maga? Is it because I'm like this now? When I was young, I wasn't dried up like you. I glowed like turmeric.'

'Parthakka, if *you* start labour pains *I'll* go and fetch the midbai,' announced Shiva.

'Why do *I* need a midbai? I might deliver the midbai's baby and send her home. Mani, do you know how I had Bhaskara?'

'Thuuu! You women and your birthing puranas. I don't want to hear them. Dirty women!' he said, finishing his breakfast and getting up.

'Ei! Who birthed you?' teased Saroja as he went out. She always stood up for women.

'How much of a man is he, anyway? It's nice to watch him show off. He's beginning to sprout a moustache but he's still climbing trees,' said Parthakka, indulgently and continued, 'When do you think I started my labour pains? The sun had not even touched the horizon. It was that early in the morning. As soon as I knew what they were I hurried through my work. I told him. We ate a handful and finished the ritual of eating. "Should I call Subbakka from up the road?" he asked. "Hm," I said. I spread a mat. I lay on it. By the time Subbakka came, the baby was already out. All she had to do was to cut the cord. If she had delayed in coming, I would've done even that.'

'Hm! A likely story! ...' said Rathna, right from where she was lying down.

'Yes, it does seem like that to women of these days, maga. To us, it was a skill. That's how *we* were. Modern girls can't do such things, I agree.'

Shiva came in after rinsing his hands clean. He was rubbing down his chest and back too, sweating after eating the steaming gruel. 'All that's fine, Parthakka. You said you'd bear as many children as you could. What if all of them had also married Shudras.'

Such a comment did not always bring sadness to Parthakka. Sometimes, it brought laughter too. That was a serious topic, no doubt. It was funny

---

[10] ganji: gruel made with rice

too. 'What can we do? But it doesn't always happen that way, does it? Just because Bhaskara did that, is there any guarantee the others too would go his way? Okay, let's say the others did. I would live just like this, accepting it as my fate.... Today, you're talking this way. Let's see what you'll do tomorrow....'

'Tomorrow's worries for tomorrow. Today, I've eaten a great breakfast of ganji. Now I have to go to school and eat Jathanna Master's caning. For not doing my maths homework,' he said as he walked out.

For ten days no one could enter Rathna's room. No one could touch her either. Not even sunlight and breeze. What about Rathna? Could she at least step out? O, no! For her bath and other washings there was an enclosure, a lean-to right behind the birthing room. They had dug a pit and set a plank on it and enclosed it with coconut palm for privacy. They had swept the afterbirth, blood and such things from the room, and buried it in that same pit. A woman called Appi did all this kind of work. She commanded great respect for doing it. If Parthakka had not been there, she would have had to stay with the new mother all those ten days. But since Parthakka happened to be there, there was no need for Appi to help in the process of Rathna's convalescence after childbirth.

'If someone dies today, the day after is already the third day' is a popular saying. It shows how fast the days fly by. It is the same with birth too. The seventh day came. The bit of dried umbilical cord dropped from the baby's navel. Gowramma showed that bit to the children. Now the baby was rid of its myligay; anyone could touch it when it was not clothed.

'Who wants to hold the baby?' asked Gowramma.

'I first! I first!' shouted Putta, Jaya, and Shami, together. But Shami had already asked on the very night the baby was born, hadn't she? So it was decided that Shami would get to hold the baby first. Parthakka took off the baby's clothes and laid her on a plank. She looked bewildered without her clothes and held out her hands and legs to clutch the air as if to get a grip on herself. The children giggled. Only little Ravi stood at the door of his mother's room that was slightly ajar, staring at her through the slit. Rathna could not bear to see him. She called out,

'Come, babanna, come here. Someone can cleanse you later by soaking your clothes and giving you a bath.'

'Stop fussing! Today he'll come and sit on your bed and tomorrow he'll come and sit right on top of your stomach. Don't pet him like that!' snapped Parthakka and turning towards Ravi said, 'Ei, you can't touch your Amma now. She's hurt herself.' Ravi was startled. He drew back the foot he had put forward and stood staring again at his mother through the opening in the door.

Gowramma picked up the baby and pretended to lay her for a while on Shami's lap. And that was it. She did the same on Putta's and Jaya's laps too. By then each one of them had touched the baby's cheeks, caressed the soles of her feet, and gushed, 'Ayyoooo! How soft she is, isn't she? Just like cotton wool! You can't even feel the touch.'

'Ravi, would you like to carry the baby? Come. Sit here,' called Gowramma but the two-year old shook his head and wet the floor. 'Si!' said Rathna, 'What's happened to this boy? It's ages since he last peed in the house. And now he wets even his bed! He needs a few slaps to set him right.'

'If I slap him, his foster-mother might tear me open. Let him pee, she'll come and wipe it. We're not supposed to scold him,' said Gowramma. The foster-mother was none other than Rathna's younger sister, Saroja, who took care of him now. Her head was full of ideals and she had a blunt way of blurting them out. Deep inside her, even Gowramma was a little afraid of this daughter.

'With her new-fangled ways, what if Saroja spoils him? What if I lose my hold on him?' murmured Rathna. Saroja came there to see what was happening.

'What's your problem?' she asked her elder sister, 'Is it because you'll have to say, "How well she looked after him! She didn't beat him even once!"? The child is already bewildered. You'll make him a moron. What if I pet him and spoil him a bit as long as he's here? Anyway, Bhavayya will sort him out when he goes home.'

Rathna wanted to retaliate but Parthakka stopped her, 'A new mother shouldn't talk too much. Lie down quietly. And don't keep chewing on what she said.' Rathna's eyes filled with tears.... But were the tears really because she was reminded of her husband? Rathna never smiled whenever she thought of him.

That night they left a pencil, a sheet of paper, a little rice, a few betel leaves and areca nuts, and some bananas, thus completing the ritual of leaving these things for Brahma to come and write the fate of the baby on her forehead. Whatever it was that Brahma wrote all the items left for Him would be given the next day to the Madivalthi[11] who washed the clothes Rathna had worn during childbirth.

---

[11] madivalthi: washer woman

two

Parthakka

Rathna was ritually purified on the eleventh day after the baby was born. On that day, her mattress and blanket were aired. Her room was washed with water. Every corner and even the cross-beam of the ceiling were sprinkled with panchagavya to be purified. At last the unclean period was over.

'O! Rathnakka's promoted from a mattress on the floor to the cot!' teased her siblings.

As for the baby, she knew nothing about madi or mylige, about being clothed or naked. All she knew was to cry when hungry and to sleep off while sucking at the breast. Sometimes she smiled in her sleep; that was for God. These days, she had also learnt to open her eyes for a while and look at the light. Tiny eyes, like pods of garlic.

Even as Vasudevaraya and Gowramma were having a discussion, 'When Ravi was born we named him on the eleventh day. Many people had come from Rathna's husband's family for his namakarana.[1] It was as grand as the celebration on the eve of a wedding. This time, there is no need to have a festivity in our house.... After all, we've had it once. Don't we have other daughters? If we don't do for them all that we've done for this one, won't there be misunderstandings ...?' There was a letter from Rathna's husband to her, '... I shall come as soon as the baby

[1] namakarana: naming ceremony

is three months old. Let them have the namakarana then.' And so, that evening they had only the ceremony of laying the baby in the cradle for the first time. All those who were invited were served coffee and some snacks. The midwife and the washerwoman were also asked to attend. Apart from the coffee and snacks, Gowramma gave them some money as well. Only the two of them washed their plates and glasses and left soon after. The others stayed on.

Gowramma herself put some baje-benne[2] on the baby's tongue. Shiva, as the baby's maternal uncle, did puje to the shining brass cradle and broke a coconut.

'O, Shiva bhattare,[3] please give us some theertha,' teased Putta in a sing-song voice.

'Oho, look at him calling Shiva a priest!' giggled one of the ladies.

Shiva rose to the occasion.

'Let the dakshine come,' he said, in a voice to match.

'If you want some dakshine,[4] please turn towards dakshina,'[5] shot back Putta.

Everyone laughed at his wit. 'How clever to play on the words! As if a purohit will get an offering if he turns towards the south,' said someone.

'It's all fine to be smart. But he still sucks his thumb!' countered someone else.

'So what if he sucks his thumb? He'll learn some day.' Saroja took his side.

'Mani, your teeth will stick out and your upper lip will become crooked. Then, no girl will marry you,' said another.

'I'll marry a man,' retorted Putta.

'Instead of telling them you'll carry off a beauty and marry her, what kind of talk is this, mani?' scolded Parthakka.

Gowramma and Rathna, seated on either side of the decorated shiny brass cradle handed gundappa, a stone pestle wrapped in cloth, to each

---

[2] baje-benne: a paste of nutmeg in butter

[3] bhattare: priest ('re' being a term of respect added to Bhatta)

[4] dakshine: offering

[5] dakshina: the south (the boys are playing on the similarity in the sound of the words)

other round the cradle from above to below to above to below ... and laid it in the cradle hoping the child would grow as strong as the stone. Then Putti too was passed the same way thrice round the cradle and laid in it. Her head was placed in a ring of soft cloth with tiny bolsters, also of cloth, on either side so that the head would grow into a nice round shape. Five muthaidhes stood on either side of the cradle and rocked it gently, singing songs to bless the newborn.

The next morning, when some salt, mustard, and pepper corns were circled round the baby and tossed into the embers they spluttered sending out such an acrid smoke that everyone in the house had a fit of coughing. 'What a pungent smell! See how much of the evil eye had to be drawn out of the baby!' the elders said.

Rathna's bananthana[6] continued. Previously during such convalescence after birthing, Parthakka would have seen to the new-mother's oil-baths, but now that she did not have the energy, Gowramma appointed Chandu to help out for twenty rupees a month. She would give her a new sari after the three months. But it was Parthakka who bathed the baby. She had prepared some herbal oil to massage her by crushing a red root in oil and heating it. The baby gurgled at the sunlight during the massage but how she screamed when she felt the warm water! All the neighbouring houses could hear her. Putta, Shami, Jaya, Shiva, and even Saroja rushed to the bathroom. Each of them comforted her in their own way, 'Over, Putti. It's al...most over.... What happened to our little babu? ... We'll brand the one who's giving you a bath with a red hot iron rod, shall we?' But, of course, Putti did not stop crying until her bath was over. Parthakka brought the baby into the bedroom, wiped her head, and wrapped it in a strip of soft cloth, wiped her face and every fold in her neck, armpits and thighs, and powdered her all over. Fondling and kissing her, she crooned, 'Hm, now my little Ammu can go to the market!' or something equally silly. Every day, before laying the baby in the cradle she asked Rathna, 'You've nursed the baby before the massage, haven't you?' The children's lips were in a perpetual pout with petting and kissing the baby. As for Putti, she went into a deep slumber as soon as she was laid in her bed after the warm bath. Even then, Putta, Jaya, and Shami

---

[6] bananthana: period of convalescence after birthing

crowded around the cradle, gave her cheek a soft peck and said, 'We're off to school now. Be awake by the time we get back, mari.'

After Putti went to sleep, Rathna went for her bath in the kela-kone. While the bananthi[7] sat on a plank in the lean-to, Chandu massaged the new mother with oil, feeding her neighbourhood gossip for well over an hour. Sometimes, milk squirted from Rathna's breasts. 'Look! The baby must've sucked on its lips in the cradle. This happens when the baby is hungry,' was Chandu's explanation as she caught the milk in her cupped hand. There is a belief that a mother's milk should not spill to the floor.

If Chandu spent hours oiling and massaging the bananthi, who was to tend the fire? How would the bath-water stay hot? What was the point in bathing her in tepid water? Gowramma's anger rose to her head. 'If the bananthana is compromised, the mother will have to suffer all her life with aches and pains,' she called out to Chandu. Even Rathna was not spared, 'Where's the need for such pointless chatter? That Chandu, of course, doesn't know about such things. But don't you know better? Did you think your mother would grow younger by the day? My back is broken. Am I to see to things in the house or outside?' And then to Chandu again, 'Sitting in so much of smoke for so long, the bananthi might lose her eyesight.'

'Where's the smoke? I've got only two hands. Can't someone else see to the fire?' Chandu too could get angry.

'Why, are you Brahma to have four hands? If we work efficiently, why do we need even the two we have? Just one should do. You haven't yet given the cattle anything to drink, haven't yet taken out the dung from the cowshed. You haven't yet washed a single cooking vessel. Will all this be done if you sit massaging her and unravelling stories about everyone in the neighbourhood?'

Chandu came out. She was known for her sharp tongue anyway. So now, the fight gathered force. Parthakka, who had been watching all this while, sent a barb from her corner of the verandah, 'If people who have to slog for a few grains of rice can spit out so much bile, what about people like us?'

---

[7] bananthi: the new mother

'What sort of talk is this, Amma?' fired Chandu, 'It is enough to pierce the heart and come out from the back. I don't want to work here. I can't do it. Get someone else from tomorrow.'

'Go right now. Do you think we can't do it? Are you working for free? Or do we pay you only the salary? Let's see who else will give you your meals and snacks and also pay you as much as we do.'

'I'll go. Do you think there's no other house around? For the way *I* work, there're people who'll beg me to work for them.'

'Fine, you have houses to work in and we have people to work for us. The more gracious we are, the more arrogant these people become.'

Chandu got up and walked away. The fire in the bathroom had burnt itself out. Rathna, smeared in oil, called out, 'Amma, what kind of fate is this? My eyes are burning. I'll bathe now.'

'Wait, maga,' said Parthakka and relit the fire. The water became hot. She herself poured hot water on Rathna, bending her aged body. As Rathna came in from the bathroom, Parthakka bound her waist tight to shrink her stomach, gave her a glass of hot milk and said as she did every day, 'Soon after you drink this, cover yourself and lie down. Let your body sweat. It's good for a bananthi to sweat.' And she closed the windows and door as no light or air was to touch the new mother. In a little while the baby got up; it was that late.

Venka who worked in a neighbouring house came over and helped them out, saying she would work for them until they got someone else. She did not have to cook for the next two days; she had a bellyful of stale rice, fresh rice, and coffee. She told Gowramma, 'Amma, I met Chandakka in the fish market. She mocked me saying, "These good times won't last for long." That Chandakka has no sense. How could she leave such a golden house! She'll soon be sorry.' And in return, she got some boiled and dried jackfruit seeds and a coconut shell of pickles.

Two days later, Venka brought Rukku to work for them.

'Do whatever you're asked to do. Don't talk back. Amma will look after you well,' Parthakka told her.

Parthakka had come to live in Vasudevaraya's house quite some time ago and she was considered a member of the family. Bhaskara was barely four when Parthakka's husband died. She had brought him up with some 200 kg of rice a year that came to her from her father-in-law's house for their livelihood; she did not seek anyone's help. When Bhaskara left home to continue his studies, Vasudevaraya asked Parthakka to move in with them.

'Where's the need for you to cook and eat alone like a ghoul?' he said to her, 'Come and live with us. Gowri tires easily these days. You could help her out.'

Previously, whenever she had guests, Gowramma used to ask Parthakka to come and help her with the cooking and now, she had become a member of the household. She had been a great help when Gowramma's last few children were born. Who could bathe a bananthi like Parthakka? Who knew how to give the newborn an oil bath like her?

But of late—ever since Bhaskara got married—she had lost her zest for life. He used to say he would never marry. Eventually he did, when he was touching forty and without telling anyone. Parthakka could not talk about that wedding. As soon as she heard about it she said, 'Vastheva,[8] now my bond with your home is broken. Let me live elsewhere and die. I don't want to live here and be a black spot during auspicious ceremonies. You're yet to celebrate the weddings and the upanayana[9] of your children.' But Vasudevaraya would not hear of it.

'Whatever is written in our children's foreheads will happen to them. How can we predict such things? You stay on; whatever will happen, will happen. Let me worry about what people say,' he said.

But Gowramma had felt it would be better to let Parthakka go. 'Who will face the people tomorrow? This is a good time. Let us send her away now. She won't feel bad about it, nor should we,' she said to her husband when they were alone.

'What sort of a woman are you? You're like those people who say, "Where's the need for the boatman?" after they've crossed the river,' he scolded her. 'If I send her away now, who'll call me a human being?'

'I know about all that. I'm not that stupid. But we do have a responsibility to get the children to the other shore, don't we? Have you thought of *that*?'

---

[8] Vastheva: mispronunciation of Vasudeva

[9] upanayana: an initiation rite to confirm a Brahmin boy in the dharmic, vedic way of life

'The way you're talking, it sounds as if only *you* are worried about them. Once I've said Parthakka will stay, the matter is closed. We don't need to discuss this again.'

Gowramma could not speak a word. But she was simmering, 'Did *I* say I didn't want Parthakka? Can I ever repay her in this life for all she's done for me? But once we're born as human beings we do have such things as paapa[10] and punya,[11] don't we? If we keep her with us, what if the flood of Bhaskara's evil deed sweeps us away together with his mother? We could repay our debt to her in another way; we could keep her in another house and yet look after her.' Though she could think of so many ways of telling her husband these things, she could not talk to him.

The days went by, Gowramma got used to the situation. Though the problem did bother a corner of her mind now and then, she could not have sent away Parthakka even if her husband had suggested that she should. And so, in a relationship that was both caring and uncaring the days rolled by.

Of course, wherever people met, whether it be by the wells or on the front porches of each other's houses or within the inner courts of the temple, they criticized Vasudevaraya for sheltering Parthakka but none of them had the courage to confront him.

That year there were so many jackfruits one could barely see the leaves. The fruits had ripened early too. Usually, they matured closer to the monsoon. Then they were neither ripe enough to eat nor raw enough to make happala. And who'll eat the jackfruit of the rainy season? So they were given away to just about anyone who came by.

But that season seemed auspicious; the fruits had ripened in time. 'But this is also a busy time for the family,' fretted Gowramma, 'I have to cook the bananthi's diet besides cooking for the family. Am I a young girl to see to the jackfruit too? I can't carry on like this. That Parthakka has been muttering hara, hara[12] under her breath. Why

---

[10] paapa: sin, wicked deeds
[11] punya: virtue, good deeds
[12] Hara, Hara: chanting the name of God (Lord Shiva)

would she call on God is she didn't feel she was getting on in years? She doesn't work with verve these days but, at least, she does her bit through habit. That's how I've been able to cope. Though there's hardly any strength in her body and no zest in her spirit, Parthakka isn't the sort who will just sit about and eat without helping out as much as she can. When I get as old as Parthakka, they may have to carry me about; I'll be completely useless.'

'Get the jackfruits from the tree. Rukku can cut open a raw one. Is it a big job if the children help out? There's nothing much to be done to make happala,' said Parthakka, trying to enthuse Gowramma.

That was true enough. And besides, the children had been on vacation for the past two days. They had been out of control, running around the yard and wilting in the blazing sun. Whenever they had holidays, Gowramma felt she had to drink a decoction of at least a seer of pepper corns to soothe her throat; she was that hoarse with shouting at them. Fortunately this year, Saroja took charge of them; they listened to her at least. 'But how do we get someone to get the fruit from the tree?' grumbled Gowramma, 'Do Shudras come to the door looking for work as they used to? They think no end of themselves. Why, that Sadiya used to come till recently to loosen the soil around the plants. Now he has rings on two of his fingers and oils his hair and combs it back! But how does it help? A Shudra is a Shudra, after all. They don't know that. At least Govinda used to come when sent for. Now, he's working at the tile factory. Even Bachcha went away to the hills to work in the areca plantations. We haven't been able to get labourers for odd jobs ever since the tile factory came up. They won't work for us however much we're willing to pay them. This is getting to be too much.'

Just when Gowramma was telling Parthakka, as she did every year, that she would give the tree on lease, Manja arrived on the scene. He was always very obliging; he did as he was told. He was grateful for favours. He was too scared of the cold to go to the hills and he was not interested in working at the tile factory. He spent his time doing odd jobs like cleaning out the base and the crown of coconut trees, plucking jackfruit and pruning flowering plants.

'Manja, good you came! Look at you! You've come as if I had sent for you,' said Gowramma.

'That's what a relationship is all about, isn't it, Amma? What do you want me to do? Tell me,' replied Manja. Flapping the towel hanging from his shoulder and tying it round his head, he stood with a hand on his hip.

For Manja, lowering the jackfruits from a tree was as easy as lowering a pot into a well.

'In your last life, you must've been a manga.[13] That's why you clamber up like a monkey. In this life you're Manja,' said Shiva.

'Whatever you say is right,' laughed Manja. Gowramma was generous while paying him. She gave him some coffee and snacks as well.

'Come after two days. The mangoes in the wild mango tree will be ready to be plucked. The well needs to be desilted. You know how to clean the well, don't you?' she asked.

'What, Amma? What a question to ask! For a man who lives by his labour, is there something he can do and something he can't?' Manja sat under the Bimbala tree, smoking a beedi.

The next day, Rukku selected a ripe jackfruit from the pile. It was an arm long. Keeping it on a palm-mat, she slashed it open with a cleaver. 'Agaa, Parashurama!' shouted Shami. The children standing around Rukku, laughed. Rukku too giggled; one of her slashes missed its aim.

'Shamamma, go away from here for a while. You're not letting me work,' said Rukku, touching her nose-ring. With a few more deft strokes she hacked the jackfruit into eight pieces.

'That'll do,' said Parthakka, 'Now, go and see to the housework. Don't touch the pods of fruit. I'll call you after they've been taken out. Come then and cut up the thin white strips and inner stem into small pieces before giving them to the cattle with rice water. Or else they'll choke and die,' said Parthakka.

'Oho? So, I'm good enough to cut open the jackfruit for you but not madi enough to touch the pods you eat! You're clever, aren't you, Parthakka? That's why your son did what he did,' grumbled Rukku, standing apart on a parapet by the cowshed. She comforted herself by opening her pouch, smearing sunna on a betel leaf and stuffing it into her mouth while crunching a betel nut.

[13] manga: monkey

Where were the children when you wanted them to pull out the fruits from the fibre? They were all there till then, watching Rukku and getting in her way. But when they were needed, there was not one except little Ravi, smeared with oil before bath and circling one of the pillars on the porch.

'They want hapla to eat during the monsoon but now they're playing truant,' complained Parthakka. 'That's why I told you not to take this on. Did you really expect the children to help out? Not one of them has any sense of responsibility. Wait a moment. Saroja is the right person to handle them. She'll fetch them,' said Gowramma going indoors. By the time she came out again, the children had gathered from that corner and this, from the edge of the large backyard and the alleyway in the small backyard. And they sat in a row, subdued.

'I want a spoon. I can't take out the pods with my fingers,' said Putta.

'Why? What's so special about you? Was your cradle tied in the attic? I too want one,' asked Jaya.

'Don't fight,' Parthakka scolded them, 'Don't you want anything else? Let's see how well you can take out the pods with your fingers. You'll use the spoons and forget to take them in and then the crows will take them away. Can we always keep an eye on the servants?'

Shiva had to put in his bit, 'I don't mind giving him a spoon. Otherwise, we'll have to eat haplas mixed with the thumb-sucker's enjalu throughout the monsoon.'

In a flash, Putta pulled out his thumb, came over to Shiva and pinched him.

'Shiva, did you have to tease the boy sitting so quietly? What is this enjalu you're talking about? The spit of children below eight is the spit from the mouth of God himself; it doesn't pollute. Putta, go and wash your hands, mani. Why do you have to listen to such things from him?' Putta washed his hands and came and sat down. In the kitchen, Gowramma stood before the fire cooking while Saroja helped her with the chopping and grinding.

Though there was some starting trouble with getting the fruit from the fibre of the jackfruit, the work chugged along steadily as they shared stories and sang songs. Parthakka sang songs about Krishna being laid in the cradle and of Draupadi's *vasthraapaharana*.

And no one could narrate ghost stories as well as Parthakka.

She told them of the Ankadhakatte ghosts that danced on full moon nights with nothing on, not even the ududhaara, 'One full moon night, Kodi Sitarama had no choice but to walk down that very road. That's when the spirits saw him. But Sitarama was clever; he took off his mundu and shirt quickly, tossed them aside and danced with them, just like them. Only after they disappeared as the day dawned did Sitarama put on his clothes and reach home safely. For eight days after that he had a raging fever; it was touch and go with him. But would he have survived if he hadn't done what he did? He would have surely died. Only his bones ... that's all ... only his bones would've been left.

'There were so many spirits of that kind. Early one morning when Antha was walking to work, a ghost taller than the sky followed him. Antha walked quickly without turning back even once. He guessed it was a female ghost; he could hear the tinkling of anklets. It could not touch him as he kept repeating, "Rama Rama," the whole way.'

Then there was a story about a spirit in the High School grounds! This was from Shiva's gazette, 'Once when Appu, the driver, was driving late at night, a ghost stopped the car. "Give me a beedi," it said. He offered one. It fell down because there was a hole in the ghost's hand; whatever was given to it fell to the ground. "Pick it up for me," said the ghost. Appu knew that if he bent to pick up the beedi, the spirit would whack him on the back and make him spew blood. So, he didn't pick it up. Instead, he said, "Look up!" And when the ghost lifted up its head and looked at the sky, Appu sped away from there.'

The children listened with rapt attention whether they could follow the stories or not. They could hardly breathe. Little Ravi was also with them.

'We must be as brave as Appu,' said Putta.

'What're you saying?' countered Shiva, 'He stopped the car and he gave it a beedi. He shouldn't have done that. Had I been there, I would've sped away from that place.' Ravi, watching Shiva's histrionics, clapped.

'It's not all that easy, mani. When a ghoul stops the car, it looks like you and me, that is, like normal human beings. Then it holds on to the handle of the car and grows to its size. Then what can you do?' asked Parthakka.

'Sarojakka said the ghosts are just make-believe,' added Jaya.

'Yes, of course. Ghosts are make-believe until you see them,' was Shiva's comment.

The children shivered.

While they were deep in such conversation, a stench stung their nostrils. They turned round, looking for the source. It was the thoti. She was walking by with a basket of shit on her head. 'Uvve!' Putta said in disgust. Shiva held his nose and said, 'What a stink!' It sounded as, 'What a stig!' because he was pinching his nose. The other children started imitating him. When they got too boisterous, Parthakka scolded them, 'Stop it, children. Monkeys too imitate one another, don't they?' And then to the scavenger she shouted, 'Hey, you dead woman! Couldn't you have come at any other time? Do you have to come at the auspicious moment when we're pulling out the pods from the jackfruit? Do you want us to feel sick and throw up?' Parthakka moved a little to block the bowl of fruit from the woman's eyes.

'If her eyes fall on the fruit, we'll have to forget about it. She belongs to the evil-ridden community, after all! Dirty people!'

'How is she dirty, Parthakka?' asked Putta.

'If not dirty, is she holy? What's she carrying on her head? Shit from whichever house! And the stench from all of it is coming to *our* noses. Thu! And I've even had my bath.'

The children felt she was right; they could not bear the stink. They added their voices too.

'If only human beings didn't have to do such a disgusting thing!' said Shiva.

'Then the thoti will die without work,' remarked Parthakka.

Rukku, who was filling the cauldron with water, heard her and murmured, 'Why will she die if she marries someone respectable?' and with a knowing smile disappeared into the bathroom. Parthakka's face fell instantly as she shot her a glance. She had felt many times that Rukku should be sent away; she was getting too impertinent. But if they stopped her, could they get another servant?

However, she had gone too far this time. She had to be put in her place. She could leave if she wanted to. Was the proverb, 'If one who eats bran goes away, the one who eats chaff will come in his place,' made for nothing? And so, Parthakka took her to task. Initially, Rukku gave back as good as she got, but soon she began to wonder what had got into her. 'Leave what you're doing and get out right now,' she heard Parthakka saying. 'I should've minded my business and done the dishes. It's my fate to have to listen to such things. But whose face did I see this morning to hear them today?' wondered Rukku, weeping silently as she carried pots of water to fill the cauldron in the bathroom. She was not like Chandu who could hit just once to break anything into two pieces; Rukku hung on to her tears, blaming herself.

Though Gowramma heard them quarrelling, she did not step out. She felt for Parthakka, 'What arrogance in people who toil to eat! How could she say such things to Parthakka! Rukku was wrong.' But then, she was also irritated, 'Anyway, how can Parthakka ask her to leave right now? Is my grandfather here to help me out? First, she sent away Chandu. Now, if this one too leaves, who'll work for us? A great help she is indeed, sending away servants from a home where there's loads of washing to be done and cauldrons of water to be filled! But can I open my mouth and talk about it? Parthakka might get upset. These things are enough to choke anyone; they can't be swallowed, they can't be spit out. But I brought this upon my head, didn't I? I must get a moment with Rukku and talk to her. After all, she said what she did only because Parthakka's son has done what he's done. Otherwise, would Rukku have the courage to speak the way she did? What's the point in scolding her?'

Rathna too peeped out of the window of her room to watch the fight. Only Saroja continued to churn the buttermilk, chanting the Achhyuthaashtaka in praise of Krishna to its rhythm; she did not want to hear the squabble.

The fruit was boiling. The children were told they could play until they were called to help out again. And so they were in the little room below the lower attic. Gowramma went to Rathna in the bananthi-room and said, 'Why should she tell ghost stories in a house with a bananthi? This Parthakka hasn't matured with age. It's the bananthis that ghosts enter. You've got a knife with you, haven't you?'

'Hm,' replied Rathna. There was no zest in her voice, fear had spread over it.

'Wherever you go, whether to the bathroom or the toilet, carry it with you. It's a mutsu that keeps away evil spirits.'

'Hm.'

Saroja was folding the baby's clothes right there. She was amused.

'Akka,' she said to her elder sister, 'Where's the need to be scared? Amma says such things because she was raised in such a set-up. But you can think for yourself, can't you?'

Rathna stared at her sister; she did not speak a word. But were her eyes saying, 'You wait until the day you have your baby when you'll be lying in bed, looking pale and feeling half-dead. Then *I'll* see if you're scared of ghosts or not.' Saroja laughed again.

'Saroja talks as if she's someone important. She tries to copy Bhaskaranna's ideas. None of them are her own,' complained Rathna to her mother a little later.

'Do you think I don't know?' said Gowramma, 'I understand everything. She thinks too much of herself. If Bhaskara did what he did, it was okay. But can she do the same? She's neither here nor there. The day I hand her over to someone, I'll feel I've won.'

That day, the task of making the hapla went on quietly. When Vasudevaraya came home in the evening, the children reported the events of the day to him. 'Why does Rukku have such a long tongue?' he said. On hearing that, Rukku sat at the door of the cattle shed and sobbed. When Parthakka was busy elsewhere, Gowramma went to Rukku and consoled her, 'Now, stop whining! You needn't have brought this on yourself. Why did you have to talk to her like that? Who is she and who are you? Anyway, what is said is said. Don't do it again. Don't feel bad that she scolded you. Who's paying you your salary and keeping you here? Isn't it us? Did we say anything to you? Don't tear up your umbrella for a single rain.' She spoke to her gently and gave her a measure of broken-rice. Or else how could she be sure the woman would come to work the next day? No one else may need such people, but she did, didn't she?

Before the end of the day, the Koosa woman who brought fresh grass for the cattle was also given some jackfruit seeds and fruit.

'In your eagerness to put away the fruit, did you miss count and give us a few bundles less?' Gowramma checked.

'No, never, Amma!' the Koosa protested, 'I've given you as many as I always do. It's getting more and more difficult to get fresh grass. I have to get it from long distances. Today, I'm dead tired just putting so much together. It's only because it's your house that I give so much.'

She was pregnant again. Wonder how many times she has been pregnant. It seemed like one long pregnancy. If she was not pregnant she was nursing a baby. Besides the job of carrying loads of grass, she had the job of carrying a baby in her womb. But she was not tired of having babies. She always said, 'Do we have to feed them, odathi? Don't we have people like you? They'll survive somehow.'

Her younger brother had a good job. He was the only educated person in the Koosa community. But he never asked her whether she was alive or dead. Was she good enough to match his status? So, she did not visit him either, nor did she send her children over.

Quite recently he had come to Vasudevaraya's house to see him about something. Vasudevaraya had never been very particular about madi and mylige, anyway. He had not given up the practice, nor had he held on to it. His was the middle path. Pretty soon after the guest arrived, Shiva came to his mother and announced, 'Appayya wants two glasses of coffee.'

'Who's come, mani?'

'I don't know. He looks very dark. He's wearing a clean white shirt like the ones fresh from the dhobi.'

Gowramma set the water to boil and peeped out. And then she came to Parthakka and said, 'That's the Koosa's brother!' as if asking, 'What shall I do now?'

'What! How can you serve *him* coffee? Is that Vastheva growing immature with age?'

Vasudevaraya himself came in. 'What is this? Are you wondering if you can serve him coffee? So what if he's a Koosa. Send it quickly.' He spoke as if it were an order.

'He must've got suspicious. See how he came in to tell us,' whispered Gowramma as she mixed the coffee.

Parthakka did not think it was right at all. As Shiva took the coffee to his father's room, Parthakka went with him up to the verandah and said, 'Don't touch *his* hand while offering him coffee. Give it to him from a distance. It's okay even if you leave his glass on the table.'

a dependent? In a way, I would've been the dependent trying to manage the household, had you not been here.'

'If you talk this way, you're insulting me. Didn't I say right at the beginning that I was raising the issue only for the sake of argument? I don't have to tell you again and again what respect you command here, as Bhaskara's mother,' said Vasudevaraya and went back to his room.

three

Bhaskara

Parthakka felt as if someone had shaken her awake every time she was reminded of her son, Bhaskara.

She went to the bananthi's room and saw Rathna seated, leaning against a wall holding a book, and warned her, 'Don't sit for too long. You'll start a backache tomorrow. What will happen to your eyes if you read like this?'

'Go on, Parthakka. I'm tired of lying down all the time.'

'Now you'll be bored. But in another three months, you'll be longing to lie down. Your back will ache that badly, your eyes too, and your whole body. Listen to me, maga. You shouldn't neglect your bananthana. Go and lie down.'

Rathna put away the book.

The baby was sleeping deeply after her bath. She was resting her arms on either side of her head, her fists clenched. 'See how the baby's sleeping! Doesn't she look as if she's carrying a basket of mud? People say, when a baby is in the darkness of its mother's womb, it cries out to God, "O God, please get me out of this darkness." And God asks, "What will you give me if I do?" And the baby says, "I'll build you a temple." Now it has come to the earth, hasn't it? It has seen light, hasn't it? Now God comes from time to time and keeps saying, "You haven't done a thing for me." That's when the baby smiles in its sleep, for it says, "O, I'll surely build you a temple" and keeps sending Him away. It starts building the temple when it's about two to two and a half months old. This is the way it carries loads of mud. Open out her palms and look. You'll find bits of dirt in them.'

Rathna nodded. Parthakka had told her the same story when Ravi was born, she remembered. And now she was repeating the story. She would surely tell it all over again when Saroja in turn had *her* baby. But Rathna could not bring herself to say, 'You've told me this story, Parthakka.' Such stories were always like that; stories about babies were all like that. They got tastier every time you heard them. She did not want to go to the sleeping baby, open her clenched fists, and look for the dirt because she did not want the story to lose its sense of mystery.

'I'll lie down,' she said, resting her head.

'You shouldn't look at your baby while she's sleeping. You'll cast an eye on her,' cautioned Parthakka as she let down the mosquito net over the cradle and sat down beside it, rocking it gently. With the rocking, her thoughts went back to Bhaskara.

'How old do you think our Bhaskara was when my husband died? Barely four years old. I used to rock his cradle this way until he was six. Did I have any other world then? How many songs I've sung for him! Now, I don't remember even half of them ... After all that, he's made me suffer so much. When I think of it, I feel as if my gut is being sliced in two.'

Rathna listened to her with compassion. 'Don't feel sad, Parthakka,' she consoled her, 'What can be done? These things are written on our forehead, aren't they?' She spoke like an elder, as if she had learnt the lines by heart.

'How can I not feel sad, tell me? I keep remembering him whatever else I may be doing, whether I'm sitting or standing. Do you know that?'

At that moment Saroja too joined them. 'What're you talking about, Parthakka? I came in to listen to you. Oh, it's about Bhaskaranna as usual!'

'Hm, yes, it's about your Bhaskaranna as usual! What else has this Parthakka to talk about if not about him? The way you talk makes me wonder if I'm the old woman or you. Wonder when you'll give up that tone of arrogance!'

'Ayyayyaa, I wasn't being insolent now!'

'...'

'Whatever you may say, Parthakka,' continued Saroja, 'Did you give birth to Bhaskaranna hoping he would look after you later? Has Rathnakka had Ravi and this baby expecting them to listen to her when they grow up? Anyway, it's only after the baby is born that you feel a "This is mine" kind of possessive love, isn't it? And there's joy in that feeling, isn't there? You yourself say there's no match for the happiness a baby brings. After enjoying them so much, why should we count our hardship in bringing them up as if it were a loan they should pay back with interest when they grow older?'

'Maga, how old are you?' asked Parthakka in reply, 'How experienced are you? Surely, it's right for you to be talking this way at your age. Get married soon and, before you know it, you'll have a baby. Let that baby grow up. Then you'll understand what all this is about. People say we should give up such illusions. Once we give up our illusions, why do we need the world? How did I bring up my Bhaskara? Did I have all I needed, as you people do? Only God knew my difficulties; that's why I had as much milk as I did. I was able to nurse him for two years. It wasn't just to pacify him either. If he forgot to come to me, I'd call him and nurse him. I had so much milk. I didn't have sunken breasts like girls of today. What kind of breasts do you have? In four months, they've dried up. You need tinned milk and feeding bottles. Is this any way to bring up babies?'

Parthakka forgot all her grief for the moment and laughed.

Rathna too laughed. She was also embarrassed. Her hands straightened her sari to cover her breasts. Parthakka sat there without a blouse, with her red sari covering her shaven head. Even now, despite her withered state, her breasts showed signs of a lost fullness.

'Parthakka, after your husband died, how did you manage without wearing a blouse for so many years?' asked Rathna suddenly.

'O, let that be, maga! If I had spoken about it, Valmiki would've written my story instead of the Ramayana. Yes, what was I talking about? It was about Bhaskara, wasn't it? That boy kept saying he wouldn't get married and he ended up marrying a Korathi! Let him marry whoever he wants. At least, if he had come and told me, "Amma, this is the situation", even if I had got angry with him I would've consoled myself that I didn't have a son and I would've forgotten him. But God didn't give him that much of wisdom.'

Gowramma, on her way to the storeroom, murmured, 'This Parthakka has found the right kind of audience to hold forth.'

'Your mother said I wasn't dependent on outsiders,' carried on Parthakka, 'Your father too. That's their goodness. But is this where I belong? Whatever it be, it's their bounty. If I fall ill and become bedridden and mess up my bed, Gowri will have to clean it up. Is that right? Sometimes when I think of such things at night, I don't get a wink of sleep, do you know?'

'His wife is supposed to be a good woman, Parthakka. She's very hospitable to her guests. Appayya himself was telling us about it. And has Appayya just visited them a few times? He's spent quite a few days with them, hasn't he?'

'Yes, that he has! What karma does he have to fulfil by going to his house? I don't think it's proper for your father to visit them or stay with them. Why should he go there, he who wears the janivara, he who recites the gayathri japa everyday? Ask him if Bhaskara has asked him even once if his mother is dead or alive. This boy who doesn't ask about his mother is going to redeem the world, is he? Let his wife be good to him, let her serve him festive food fit for the gods, what is it to me?'

'I believe she was asking him to bring you to their house, right in front of Appayya,' said Saroja.

'Of course, she'll say that! There'll be someone to cook for them.... Maybe she asked for me. What did he who's supposed to be my son say to that? Did he say anything at all? Maybe he was scared your father may take me if he did. May he lose his tongue! May worms infest the water he touches! Vastheva will never do that to me and I'll never step into Bhaskara's house. He's *not* my son.' Her voice quivered to a whisper. At the edge of her cataract-ridden sunken eyes surrounded by wrinkled skin a teardrop trembled.

'You only have to feel you don't like something and you get so angry about it. You're really the limit, Parthakka,' said Saroja.

Rathna did not like Saroja's cutting remark. 'What is her age?' she thought, 'And what is Parthakka's? Shouldn't she rein in her tongue a bit? Who can bear the grief if her son marries a Korathi? Let him marry anyone from any other caste. But why a Korathi of all people? If my Ravi does something like that, even I, modern as I am, will surely not tolerate it. What does Saroja know? She's not married yet. She has no children. She doesn't know the fire of suffering.'

And turning on her sister, she said, 'Saroja, what's so terrible about what Parthakka says? Think about it yourself. Tomorrow if your son marries a Korathi—the lowest of all castes, the lowest of the lowest caste—and brings her to your house, will you take her in? Forget about that. Are you willing to marry a Koraga?'

'How can I answer such questions now? I'll know only when such things happen. There's no value to whatever I say now, whether I say, "yes" or "no". But, Rathnakka, Bhaskaranna's mind is not like yours or mine. His way of thinking is different. There're many people working for the welfare of the Shudhras. But, tell me, who has taken it so seriously as to marry one of them and have the courage to become a part of her life? Bhaskaranna kept saying he would never get married and yet, do you know why he married Kumudhini athigay? One day he told Sheenanna, "I didn't get married to her to redeem her. I married her because I want to be one among those who're considered the lowest of the lowest. I want to feel that I'm like them and they're like me." But poor things, her people will not let them enter their homes. It's ages since she's been to her village.'

'That's it! That's what will happen eventually. We'll be the ones who'll help them out. Our hearts may melt with sympathy for them and we might say, "Bhaskara, come home." But her people will never accept them. He doesn't know that yet.'

'Who asked us to take them in?' asked Saroja, 'He did what he could, that's all. He might yet get whatever he had hoped for. Who can tell?'

'Stop talking, you smart girl! Who knows whose house you'll turn upside down?' Parthakka had the right to scold her that way. The children never felt bad when she scolded them. There was argument and counter argument and there was also the heat of the moment. But no rancour.

'I shouldn't have talked this way now,' rued Parthakka after a while, 'Is this any way to look after a bananthi? She should've eaten a hot meal and chewed some betel leaves without a care. I know this and yet I started my purana.' Right then they heard the tinkling of anklets against the cradle.

'O, my Ammi's up! Why have you woken up, my Ammu?' crooned Parthakka rocking the cradle briskly and singing a lullaby. 'Look at the baby, Rathna. There's a raspy sound when she breathes out. She's got a cold in the chest. We must give her a spoonful of the juice of the leaves of the sambara[1] creeper mixed with a little honey. We must desiccate a betel leaf and put it on her head. Did your mother give her the suttu-maddu[2] on Thursday? That herbal medicine has to be given regularly.'

'Hm.'

As Parthakka went out to get the leaves of the sambara creeper, Gowramma came in quietly, ladle in hand, breaking some dried red chilies into it. 'Why should she curse her son like that? Let him go and die. With both hands he'll have to eat the fruit of his deeds ... someday. What he's done is not a small thing. It isn't something you can keep in your belly. If he had at least told his mother! It's like that saying, "I bore a daughter and gave her to my son-in-law; I bore a son and gave him to my daughter-in-law." The people of old who made these proverbs weren't idiots,' she said softly.

---

[1] sambara creeper: a medicinal herb
[2] suttu-maddu: herbal medicine

four

Black Magic

Never had the month of Vaishaka[1] been so hot. In the years gone by, they would by now have had at least a few showers. But that year there had been no sign of rain. The heat was searing.

Seethu had taken on the lease for watering the plants from the first of the previous month, Chaitra,[2] and she usually stopped on the first day of Vaishaka. But there was no rain. The earth at the base of plants was parched and cracked. Seethu continued only because Gowramma had asked her to carry on till they had had at least one or two spells of rain. She had asked for an increase of ten rupees that year. 'We'll have to give it. We can't bargain for ten rupees and starve the plants, can we?' felt Gowramma. As usual, the plants were not watered on the first of the month. Seethu took a holiday on the first. Usually in the summer, there would be a thunderstorm or two, bending the banana trees, snapping off twigs and branches from jackfruit and mango trees and turning them upside down and Varuna, the Rain God, would show them the leaky spots in the attic roof telling them which tiles needed to be replaced. Wonder in which other direction he had gone on tour that year!

The water in the well had dropped lower than ever. Rukku's and Seethu's hands were blistered, drawing water. The heat was unbearable.

---

[1] Vaishaka: summer
[2] Chaitra: around mid-March to mid-April, onset of summer

To those who dropped in to quench their thirst, the jaggery-water they were served was like nectar. Rathna could not bear the thirst but a bananthi was not supposed to drink too much water. Her belly would bloat, warned Parthakka and Gowramma. And so she drank just about a glass or two, sipping a little at a time throughout the day.

Manja, who had been asked to come after two days, came at last. But for what? He had been asked to come to pluck the wild mangoes when they were ready. They had been plucked, cut, and boiled. What had to be soaked in brine had been soaked. The varieties of mango pickles had been stocked in jars and now he had come.

'Why has he come *now*? Is it to be bitten by the red ants on the empty mango tree?' asked Gowramma as she stepped out of the house into the veranda.

'Amma, it mostly because I'm frightened of the ants that I didn't come to climb the tree,' confessed Manja, smiling.

'Enough about you being scared of ants! Sidda plucked them! He smeared some ash all over his body and climbed the tree.'

'Has anyone taken out the silt from the well?'

'No. But you've come alone. How can you do it?'

'I'll get help now, Amma. That's no problem.'

'Not now. Do it later in the afternoon. Get the ripe coconuts from the tree now. We haven't any coconuts in the house. Remove the husk for about ten or twelve and stock the rest in the attic. And the yellow cucumbers are ready. They have to be hung from a bamboo pole. Get some tender fronds to tie up the cucumber.'

'O, I'll see to everything,' said Manja and, with a sickle stuck in his waist, he clambered up the coconut tree in no time. 'Now it's a rupee per tree, isn't it? There was a time when I used to climb these same trees for you at a quarter of a rupee per tree. What have the days come to?' That was his indirect way of telling the lady of the house his rate as climbed up and down the trees plucking coconuts, sticking them one by one to the sharp edge of his crowbar and deftly dehusking them. The children saw the fresh palm fronds and pranced about like calves with the wind in their ears.

'Don't touch the tender leaves, children! We need them,' shouted the elders but the children pretended those words were not for them.

Putta made a watch with the length of a palm, tied it to his wrist, and swaggered about. All of them made shrill pipes that screeched. Shiva showed them how to make a snake with it. And after his demonstration, many snakes hissed about. Some of them were made to crawl on Rukku sending her into fits of screaming. On the whole, there was quite a racket. Gowramma grumbled about the teacher who had given them a vacation. By the time Manja made nooses with the fronds and stuck the cucumbers through them and tied them to the bamboo pole hung along the wooden ceiling, the household had eaten and he was called for lunch.

Manja cut a large leaf of the yam plant, washed it and put it down with the tip away from him, placed a pot of drinking water by it, and sat down at the edge of the verandah. He ate with great relish the appetising boiled rice and a curry made of tender jackfruit and drank almost three cups of buttermilk before setting to work again.

'It's such a pleasure to serve Manja. If the dishes are spicy, he doesn't bother whether his stomach is full or not; he goes on filling it,' said Parthakka to Rukku. She was separating the midrib of the coconut palms with a knife to make brooms and Rukku was hanging out some clothes to dry. She shook out a piece of cloth briskly but did not speak a word. She was grumpy whenever anyone else but she was fed a meal or given something to take home. 'Have we ever deprived her because we gave something to someone else?' thought Parthakka. But Rukku would not learn however much this was explained to her.

Around three o'clock, Manja arrived with a helper to desilt the well. He looked into it and said, 'What Amma! These days all sorts of people have pump-sets for their wells and cement rings round their trees. Why haven't you got such things yet?'

'If we have pump-sets for our well and bunds around around our trees, where should people like you find work, Manja?' Though Gowramma spoke to him quite testily, in her heart she agreed with him, 'The man of the house should think about such things. As for my husband, he's forever preoccupied with his work. Does he ever think about the house? How much can *I* see to?'

Automatically, her mind drifted towards other problems, the rising household expenses and daughters to be married. Previously, they used to get rice from the lease-holders but now they had to buy stocks. Should we not have the pradhana-devathe for all these things? The price of groceries rose by the day but the house had to be run as it always was. If she tried to stretch the money towards some expenses, there was nothing left for some others. 'I've lost my joy in life. Am I feeling this way because he's visiting Bhaskara's house?' she wondered aloud, 'My Appayya used to say it's our primary dharma to uphold our traditional practices. But in our house we desecrate every rule.'

Manja felt bad to hear her talk that way.

'Why does Ayya do such things? He should stop going to Bhaskarayya's house. Are the Koragas just a low caste? They're *such* a low caste that not just we, why, even the Koosas won't touch them. Amma, Brahmins are Brahmins. But it's not just the Brahmins; even if anyone of a higher caste than ours comes to our door, it's as if we've committed sin. If I go to a Halepaika's[3] house, the sin falls on him, not me. We can say all this to children. Can we tell a grown-up?'

'That's right, Manja. You can't talk to him; his anger perches on the tip of his nose. Anyway, I'm finished.'

'You should see an astrologer, Amma. He'll tell you if someone's cast a spell on your house.'

'One goes to an astrologer; he'll say something or the other and one returns with fear in the heart. That's why I haven't had anything to do with such people till now. What wrong have we done to anyone that they should do black-magic on us?'

'Who told you such spells are cast only on those who do bad things, Amma? If a man has learnt black-magic, he has to use it at least once a year to hold on to its power. You don't worry; I'll set everything right.'

'Manjanna, will you get started or will you just keep talking?' asked the helper.

'We've come to work, haven't we? We'll start as soon as Seethakka comes.'

Seethu, who watered the plants, had already been sent for. At last she arrived. First, water had to be drawn for the use of the household. And then, the well had to be emptied. Manja and the helper kept drawing water with two pulleys. Seethu held a pot at her waist and swung another

---

[3] halepaika: a class of Shudras

in a hand and ran about trying to water the plants as quickly as the two men drew it from the well. At times she swung pots in both hands and watered as fast as she could. And yet, she could not match their speed. Watching them, Shiva joined in the exercise. And then Shami too. The water was not rationed out that day; there was enough to cool the belly of every tree and shrub. At last there was so little water in the well that it could not be drawn out.

Manja tied one end of the rope firmly to the rod of the pulley and let himself carefully down the steps of the deep well and sent up the remaining water and silt in a bucket. The children stood around the well peering into it. Putta, Jaya, and Shami felt their hearts go daba daba. Shiva had seen this sight many times and yet it seemed a fresh experience each time. Every time the bucket came up, the children were eager to see what it had brought up from Paathaala. And sure enough, 'Sannayya, there's a pot here!' called out Manja.

'O! Shami threw it in. That's the small brass pot,' said Shiva, 'Remember, Shami? You dropped it while trying to draw water.' Shami danced about right where she was standing and grabbed the pot.

Five or six buckets of silt came up after that. 'One of my marbles had fallen in,' said Putta with his thumb still in his mouth.

'Call out!' suggested Shiva.

Putta stood on tiptoe, peeped into the well and called, 'Ai, Manja, my marble had fallen in. Look for it.'

'Really, Sannayya? Wait, I'll look for it,' called back Manja and he pretended to look for it. 'I can't find its address, Ayya.'

Everyone laughed but Putta; he sucked his thumb noisily.

Even the brass plate was found; the harivana Gowramma had dropped last Shravana when she was worshipping the well after worshipping the threshold. But the small spoon that had fallen with it could not be traced.

About ten or fifteen minutes had gone by. Suddenly Manja raised his head and called out from the well, 'Amma! O, Amma!' From a distance, Gowramma replied, 'O!'

'Amma, come closer. Come and see. You said you didn't believe in such things. Come and see!'

The children stood on tiptoe and peeped in again. Rathna, who was standing by the door, warned Shiva, 'Shiva, look at the children! What if they fall in? Shout at them, Maharaya!' Shiva slapped each of them once and made them stand at a distance from the well.

Gowramma came closer and peeped in, saying, 'What's it now?'

Together with some silt, a glass tube was coming up in the bucket. She picked it up slowly and looked at it. It had a hole at the bottom! They surely did not have a tube of that kind in the house. How did it get into the well? Who could have brought it? Gowramma was confused. Shiva turned it over and over and said, 'We have similar test-tubes in the lab in our school. But how did this reach our well?' Now Gowramma felt dizzy. Putta looked around to see who was not there. Parthakka and Saroja. Saroja was engrossed in a book and did not respond when he called. But he kept calling until she looked up. 'There's a tube *this* long in the well,' he said, measuring his hand up to the elbow. Parthakka too was roused from sleep. Putta was satisfied only after the two of them came out.

'Someone has done some black-magic. That's for sure,' said Gowramma, 'That's why there's been a scarcity of everything recently. Otherwise, why haven't there been any suitable proposals for Saroja who's ready for marriage? However much I tell him not to go to Bhaskara's house, why doesn't my warning enter his ears? Why am I so tense as to say at the end of each day, "Is the day over? Thank God, I made it!" I can't understand.' Seethu, Rukku, and the helper agreed with her vehemently. A quarter of an hour might have passed that way. 'There's more silt to be removed. Send the bucket down,' said a weak voice from the depths of the well. That was when they were shaken from their daze. The task of taking out the silt was almost done; they could see the square base of the well. They could also see fresh water seeping into it. Manja came up.

'Manja has more strength than God,' declared Putta and would not accept that there was anyone greater.

'Do you know how much power God has?' asked Jaya.

'However much it may be, Manja has more,' insisted Putta. Wasn't Manja the strong man who had carried him on his shoulders and walked three miles to the Kodi festival at Koteshwara? Shaking sugar canes to a rhythmic ghul-ghul, listening to stories, tossing puffed rice into his mouth while Manja walked in the moonlight—why, Putta could remember all that even in his dreams.

'The Agoli Manjanna in his stories is really this same Manja,' affirmed Jaya.

As soon as he came up, Manja said, 'Have you thought about what I had told you, Amma? Don't worry. I'll take care of everything.' As Gowramma paid them their wages for cleaning the well, Manja added, 'Amma, you don't have to be afraid of anything. I'll see to it. I won't tell you what I'm going to do. Or else we won't get the right results.' And he asked for a little more for the expenses before he left.

Though everyone had gone in, Shiva stood by the well, staring into it. Last year, he and his friend, Venkatesha Bhatta's son, had smuggled out the test-tube from the school-lab without the knowledge of the master. They had wanted to conduct an experiment heating potassium permanganate. If he had confessed to it, his father would have been upset. And they had not had the courage to take it back to the lab. So he had thrown it into the well when no one was looking. And now, he did not have the nerve to own up to what he had done. He felt depressed at his own cowardice. Water had started coming into the well but it was still red and muddy. It would be clear by the next day. Shiva stood there for a long while, his mind in turmoil.

That night it poured relentlessly; a regular thunderstorm. Those who had at least some rice to eat would not venture out. Parthakka and Gowramma said to each other, 'It didn't rain all these days. Did it have to rain today of all days, when the plants have had their fill of water? Even if it had come a few days earlier we needn't have paid Seethu for those days. Probably, she'll come tomorrow and feel bad to see her efforts wasted.'

The rain beat a rhythm on the roof tiles. It pattered noisily, pata-pata, on the zinc sheets and flowed down in a steady stream. Bubbles rose and fell in the front yard like the fizz in soda-water. Pages from used notebooks sailed as paper-boats down the rivulets, rushed along, and sank. The children pranced about watching them. But they could not stay out in the rain for long. Strong gusts of winds caught at the downpour, lashing it about. What if they caught a chill? Vasudevaraya got the children in and closed all the doors and windows. Every crack of thunder scared the life out of them. Parthakka opened the door slightly and threw out a sickle saying, 'Lighting won't strike the house if there's a piece of iron guarding it.'

There was no power in the house. The children sat around a bed-lamp with nothing better to do than listen to the rain. Saroja, Shiva, and the rest started a discussion.

'What a story! Why? Does the sickle have life to stop the lightning?' asked Shami.

'Parthakka, you're a bundle of superstitions,' said Shiva.

'Go on, mani, go on. What else will you say? What do you know of the world?'

'Not just that, mani,' Gowramma added her bit, 'If you're in a hurry to go somewhere, chant the names of Arjuna. Say Arjuna, Phalguna, Partha, Kireeti, and Dhananjaya; then thunder won't come anywhere near you. After all, what's rain? Isn't it Varunadeva? And lightning is Indra. When he draws his sword, it flashes. That's the lightning. Thunder is the sound of the wheels of Indra's chariot rolling along, isn't it? If it gets too scary when Indra thunders towards us with his sword flashing, all we need to do is invoke his son, Arjuna. Indra will then be happy and quieten down.'

Jaya, Putta, and Shami sat still with fear; in all that commotion, the sky might fall on them. They were afraid, no doubt, and yet they wanted their mother to keep telling them such stories and they wanted to keep listening to them.

'That's what people said in those days,' explained Saroja, 'Probably, iron has the power to absorb lightning when it strikes. That's why they say we should put out a piece of iron when there's a thunderstorm. And then, chanting the names of a brave warrior instills courage in our hearts. A bold person can go from anywhere to anywhere. And so they might've said we should remember Arjuna this way, to make us self-confident.'

'Shabash, Sarojakka! Instead of spending time at home shooing flies, look for the meaning behind such beliefs. We'll give you a Ph.D.!' applauded Shiva. Shiva's compliment raised gales of laughter.

The elders who had been sitting in the dark slipped away from there one by one. Jaya, Shami, Putta, and Ravi got even more scared and pestered Parthakka to tell them a story. 'A sparrow came and took away a grain of paddy; another sparrow came and took away another grain of paddy....' Parthakka carried on and on; the sparrows did not stop, the grains of paddy did not get over and so the story could not get over either. 'What a story, mani! My head is whirling!' she said as she ground to a halt. But she did not tell them that the thunder, lightning, and rain had oppressed her with thoughts of Bhaskara and shaken her up.

As Putta sat listening to the story, a drop of rain had fallen on his head. He did not bother much about it. But now, there was another and yet another.

'Ayyayya, it's leaking here!' he said, standing up. And not just there. There was a little pool in the other room. Shiva was already up in the attic busily fixing the leaks in the tiles by stuffing them with the tender coconut-palms Manja had cut down and helping the water to flow down the roof. Saroja held up the torch to help him. As Gowramma scooped up the water in the room into a vessel, she grumbled, 'When will all this be set right? This is written on our foreheads, is it? How many times I've said to him, "Take out the cracked tiles and get the roof repaired before the rains." Does he listen? Every year we have to do this job. All sorts of people start getting their roofs repaired right before the monsoon. Even the Shudras thatch the roofs of their houses. Even the ants and birds know when the rains start. And to think that we don't! Che! I feel like leaving home and running away somewhere for these four months.'

'It's not just the broken tiles,' said Parthakka, 'The metal gutters are cluttered with dried leaves. That's why they're blocked and can't drain out the rainwater. If you had asked Manja to clean the gutters, he would've done it and we would've had enough dry leaves to heat at least two drums of bathwater. The rainwater wouldn't have leaked into the house. If you forgot to tell him, how could *I* too forget such a thing?'

'Ha, Parthakka! We should set fire to our brains. We've forgotten to bring the dung-cakes in! They may've been washed away by now.'

Unmindful of all the havoc it was creating, the rain kept hammering down.

five

Ramayana in the Attic

'Don't go out to play today,' Shiva told the others, 'Let's put up a play.'

'O, nataka! nataka!' the children applauded the plan. They quickly clambered up to the attic and pulled everything upside down.

'What a noise! No one seems to be downstairs,' complained Rathna.

'Shiva, what's this, mani? Aren't you aware of the bananthi at home? What's all the noise in the attic?' shouted Gowramma. But no one responded. How could they? They had not heard her at all. They were busy getting the crowns, the waistband, and the ten heads of Ravana ready. Shiva was to play Rama and Jaya was Seethe. Kadu Bhatta's two daughters were Kausalye and Sumithre. Shami was Kaikeyi. The neighbour, Duggu's sons were Lakshmana and Shathrugna.

'Dasharatha?' asked Shiva.

'We don't need him. He dies, anyway,' said Putta.

'But we'll need him until he dies. You be Dasharatha,' suggested Shiva. Putta nodded.

Shiva and Duggu's boys started working on the bows and arrows, crowns, waistbands, and other paraphernalia. But what about the dialogue?

'Who doesn't know the Ramayana? Put up your hands,' said Shiva.

'Who *doesn't* know the Ramayana, he says! Ayyayya, see what he's saying,' laughed Putta with a swagger. Of course, it was certain that anyone who said he did not know the myth would lose his part.

'So? Everyone knows it. Then, say whatever comes to your mind. I don't have the time to teach you your lines. We've spent it on making crowns and things for the royal family and heads for Ravana. Will you?'

'Hoonh!' replied the cast.

'That's settled then! You've got your costumes, haven't you? This evening as soon as Appayya comes home, we'll have the play. Until then we'll be busy setting up the stage. All of you better be handy. We'll need you to fetch and carry.'

Kadu Bhatta's eldest daughter had sent sarees for her younger sisters who were to play Kausalye and Sumithre. Saroja decided that Shami and Jaya should wear Rathna's engagement and wedding sarees. She asked Rathna's permission and even before she could sleepily say, 'Hm', she had taken them out. All this happened while Parthakka and Gowramma caught a nap after lunch. Saroja remembered their elder brother, Sheena, while dressing up her sisters.

'Shiva, we could've had this play after Sheenanna's return, couldn't we? After all, his exams will be over in a few days and he'll be back.'

'Yes, yes, a fine suggestion, no doubt! By the time *he* comes home, *our* vacation will be over.'

Even as Vasudevaraya stepped into the house, Shiva went up to him, handed him an invitation and said, 'There is a play to be enacted this evening. You must kindly accept to be the chief guest.' Vasudevaraya felt like laughing to hear his son speak to him in formal Kannada as if he were an outsider.

'Certainly! I'll be honoured,' he replied equally solemnly.

'What's the hurry, mani? He's barely come in,' Gowramma scolded Shiva and sent him away.

There was a written invitation for Rathnakka too. Parthakka and Gowramma were invited orally. There was no need to invite Seethu and Rukku. And wouldn't the neighbours, Duggu's family and Kadu Bhatta's family, come anyway? Especially when their children were acting? Just the right number for an audience; it would fill the attic.

Rathna sneaked up the stairs without Parthakka's knowledge. Had she seen her, Parthakka would have shouted, 'How can you climb stairs so soon after the baby? Your uterus might slip down!' But once she was up, there was no need to fear her. Ravi was in the way, not letting Saroja dress up the female characters. Rathna had to keep him with her. Shiva too had problems dressing up the male characters; he did not know how to tie the kachche-panche to cover their legs. Even Saroja and Rathna couldn't figure it out, however hard they tried. Finally, a strip of cloth was tied round the waist and somehow tucked in at the lower back to look like the kachche-panche and Rama, Lakshmana, Bharatha, and Shathrugna were ready at last. Dasharatha too. It was decided that Putta would play the role of Ravana after Dasharatha died.

After all the charaters were dressed up, Shiva brought the gong from God's room and sounded it. It was to announce that the spectators could come upstairs. On behalf of the troupe, Saroja brought the chief guest to the attic. She went down again and brought Rathna's baby too, thinking, 'If we leave her alone, we may not hear her even if she screams.'

'Even the cow knows there's a play today, Amma. See how early Kashi's come in,' said Rukku as she quickly milked her.

'We can boil the milk later,' said Gowramma. She put it away in the kitchen and climbed the stairs with Parthakka.

Whoever had to be there was already there. Rukku and members of Duggu's family had occupied the front row. But Shiva made them sit to a side to make way for chairs for the chief guest and his family; for Vasudevaraya, Gowramma, Parthakka, and Rathna.

Tuyn! A rope was pulled, the curtain was opened and the play began. Dasharatha's old man's voice was quivering more than necessary. And not just his voice, even his hands, legs, and neck were shivering.

'Mani, don't let your voice tremble *so* much,' advised Parthakka.

'I'm an old man, aren't I?' asked Dasharatha in Putta's proper voice.

'Parthakka, don't talk to him now,' said Gowramma, trying not to laugh.

Shiva had previously told the spectators on the mat that this was not a funny play and so they sat biting their lips. Kaikeyi did nothing much but fuss about, rubbing her eyes, and tossing her hair. The dialogue developed as the characters said whatever came to their heads. The scene somehow limped along until Rama, Seethe, and Lakshmana had to leave for the forest. Shiva had told them earlier that they had to give up their crowns and waistbands to Kaikeyi and walk away with dignity.

Shiva who played Rama's role and the boy who was Lakshmana took off their crowns but Seethe moved away from them and stood aside.

Even when Shiva as Shri Ramachandra spoke to her in formal Kannada saying, 'Seethe, take off thy crown,' she would not budge. He made signs with his eyes. Duggu's son, who was playing Lakshmana, whispered in her ear. Nothing worked. At last Kaikeyi got impatient and angrily reached for Seethe's crown.

'Ayyo, I won't give up my crown,' screamed Seethe.

'O, won't you take it off? Won't you take it off?' cried Kaikeyi, trying to pull it off her head. Seethe held on to it with all her might. Dasharatha, who was supposed to have fainted, came out of his swoon and lay there watching. He was furious to see what was happening. He got up and rushed forward like Ravana.

'Will you take it off or not? If anyone goes to the forest wearing a crown, it'll get stuck in the shrubs,' he roared.

The spectators' laughter was loud enough to bring the roof down. As it subsided, Vasudevaraya said gently, 'Take off the crown and give it to her, maga. This is a play, isn't it?'

'No, Appayya, I won't. If I take off my crown and give it to her, Shamakka will have two crowns and I won't have any.' By now Jaya was in tears. Vasudevaraya went to the stage, brought Jaya with him to his seat, wiped her tears with the bairasa[1] on his shoulder and made his speech as the chief-guest, 'I'm very happy with your efforts. The play may have to be stopped midway. I feel it could be because you did not practice well enough. Learn your lines better for the next time. Try and act as natural as possible. All of us will come and watch you then as well.' Then he called the members of the cast by name and gave them each a chocolate. He gave Jaya two and went downstairs.

Now everyone started talking together:

SHIVA: But for that shani our play would've gone on so well.
SHAMI: We should never ever give that Jaya a part in a play.
PARTHAKKA: Putta, not bad for you, mani! You became a Ravana even without the ten heads.

---

[1] bairasa: towel

PUTTA: Look at this strip of heads, Parthakka! I didn't get a chance to wear it because of this ruckus.

RATHNA: Ayyo, Shami, Jaya! Where've you been sitting? I let you wear my sarees and look at the way you've stained them! Saroja, you took my sarees as if you'd look after them. Couldn't you've asked them to be careful at least? Now who'll get the stains out for me? My grandfather?

SAROJA: Why d'you have to spring on us for such a small thing? I'll clean them for you, Maharayathi!

GOWRAMMA: Abah! Are all sisters like this all over the world?

The servants of the house and Duggu's family also grumbled; they did not think it was proper for Shiva to move them from the front row to a side, 'We couldn't see a thing. Our necks hurt with all that craning.'

'Poor boys, Bharatha and Shathrugna never got to act their parts. They only got to wear their costumes,' added Duggu, feeling sad for her sons.

'If such a thing happens the next time, we won't come to watch the play,' piped up a voice from somewhere.

'Are you *that* important? Good riddance if you don't come!' Shiva found a way to vent his frustration; his play had been a farce.

GOWRAMMA: How can you talk to them like that, mani? Did you think they came to see your good looks? Stopping the play midway is bad enough. And now you're insulting the spectators as well.

SHIVA: Why d'you fly at me? Scold your spoilt little darling daughter.

GOWRAMMA: What d'you mean by my darling daughter? All of you are the same to me ... if you behave well (screwing Jaya's ear). See how you've disgraced your brother, you silly girl.

SAROJA: Amma, will you and Parthakka please go downstairs. If you get involved in their fights, tomorrow the children will be one and you'll be left alone. That's all.

GOWRAMMA: That's also true.

Rathna also went downstairs with Parthakka and Gowramma. While they were going down the stairs, Parthakka said, 'I think Shiva was right in the way he spoke. What arrogance in those Shudras! Won't the play go on if they don't come? Did they expect him to usher them to the front row and worship them with thumbe flowers? Shiva is a manly man!'

'You must've said such things to the Shudras in your previous birth. That's why in this birth your son has married a thoti,' Gowramma said, laughing.

'Let him die! Who knows how many more times he'll have to be born to be a Brahmin? The door to heaven is closed, anyway. I've no objection. Have I lost my caste? Have I ever eaten in his house?'

The baby fussed a bit as they reached the last step. 'Ammi seems to have liked their worthless play. She didn't make a sound there. Look at her now!' said Rathna.

'She must be hungry, poor thing, nurse her,' said Gowramma as she walked into the kitchen to boil the milk. And what did she see? The milk vessel was upturned and there was only some milky stickiness on the floor! 'Fine work!' she exclaimed, 'So like the proverb: loose talk destroys a home; a leak destroys a lake.'

six

Rathna's Husband

Even as Rathna completed three months of her bananthana and entered the fourth, she received a letter from her husband: 'There's an auspicious date coming up in another fifteen days. Let them have the namakarana then. I'll come for the ceremony and bring you back.'

The baby had barely learnt to turn over. She would drool, hit her head against the floor, and bawl; she could not hold her head up, not yet. If her hand got caught under her as she turned over, she would scream. And laugh when carried, with not a trace of the crying. Such a belly-filling cackle too!

'What a shame! You've got to go just as the baby's learning to look at our faces and smile.' Parthakka could voice her sadness. 'But then, a mother's house is only a mother's house, after all. How long can you stay here?'

Rathna felt strangled at the thought of having to go back to her house. Five months had gone by since she had left home to have her baby. She was not aware of how the days had slipped away here. Now she would have to get back to a lonely life; looking after the baby, handling little Ravi, cooking meals, and snacks ... Merely thinking about it was enough to shred her nerves. Her husband would get furious if she dared to say, 'Not that way but this.' Whatever he wanted would have to materialize the moment he grunted *hoonh*; she would not be able to see to the baby first even if she were crying. She could think of her only after catering to *his* 'wants' and 'don't-wants'. In case she did see to the baby, he might even push away the plate of food and walk out. He used to get into a blind rage during the early days of their marriage. He was a little better now. Rathna took comfort in the thought.

As for Parthakka, the only man who was any man at all was Rathna's husband. She would say, 'Look at the way he holds his wife in his fist! A home is a home only when the wife is in her husband's grip. Or else, is it a home? It's a hotel.' And Rathna's eyes would sparkle with pride; she was the wife of an ideal husband. But the gleam was only on the surface. Beneath it lay, unknown to Rathna, the burden of fear, of restrictions, of suffering. Gowramma, the womb that had begotten her, could see it. But she was not one to sort out such things.

Gowramma had come to terms with her daughter's situation with, 'That's how it is with every woman. It's a package she brings with her at birth. Can she cope if she gets upset about such things?' At least if Rathna had complained about her husband, perhaps she would have given it a thought. But she had not brought even one problem to her mother, not till now. Rathna gave the impression that her husband was all she could desire; she regarded his short-temper as a manly embellishment. Would there be any point in shaking her up, probing and unsettling her? Joy or sorrow, where are they *not* found? Everything has to do with a person's karma. Even Brahma cannot wash away our karma, they say. We have to stand firm in the saying, 'Ultimately, if the result of my action is so powerful, what can you do, O God?' If He can give us the strength to wear out our karma, that should do. Whatever it be, Rathna's husband did not stint on food and clothing, he had a good job, he knew what it was to be respectable. What more could they ask for?

They had only to look around to see how fortunate Rathna was. There were so many others suffering in so many ways. That Kamalamma's daughter, Sarala, for instance. Wasn't she exactly the same age as Rathna? She had been looking like a ghost ever since she got married. Her mother-in-law was a roaring fire, enough to rage through a three-piece clay oven. After bearing two children, Sarala looked as if she was good for nothing. And yet the poor girl would always reply, 'Nothing', whenever anyone asked her, 'What's happened to you, maharayithi?' She won't talk about her troubles. She knows what respectability is. And then, what about Rathna's classmate, Padma—the one who used to flit about as if she were the world's prettiest maiden? After sitting at home refusing this man and that as if no one was good enough for her, what kind of a person did she eventually marry? One look at his face and even a dog would turn away from his food. Remembering these girls, Gowramma thought Rathna's husband was a thousand times better; keeping his house in order, buying only what was needed, and maintaining discipline at home.

But if Rathna or anyone else praised that man, Saroja would walk away from there. She could not ask them not to appreciate him. He was her brother-in-law, after all, wasn't he? Who knows? This very Rathna might complain to her husband that Saroja had spoken ill of him.

Saroja remembered how once when she had gone to her sister's house she had heard her brother-in-law shouting at her sister, 'Why have you made chutney to go with the chapaatis? Why didn't you cook a vegetable dish? Did I bring the vegetables to plaster them on your head?' He had flung the plate with the chapaatis at Rathna in Saroja's very presence and walked away. And then, until he left for office he had scolded her as much as he could; grumbling about the same thing over and over again. Yet, all that Rathna had done was to protest in a whimper, 'I'll make a vegetable dish the next time. Is that a problem? If you had told me earlier, I would've made it, wouldn't I? Where's the need for you to get so angry?' She had whined so he would not hear her. Ssi!

And that afternoon, when she had to send his lunch in the tiffin-carrier, Rathna had remembered to make a fresh vegetable dish to go with piping hot chapaatis. She had also made a few more side-dishes and sent them with the rice. Saroja's blood had boiled at that.

'In your place, I wouldn't have sent him any lunch. He would've had to go to a restaurant,' she said, unable to control herself.

Rathna had not liked the way her sister had spoken. What kind of a woman would she be if she too got angry because her husband had lost his temper? She was peeved. 'I'm not you, am I?' she had said.

Was Saroja the kind who would take that quietly? 'It's not that easy for you to be *me*,' she had retorted.

It was not unusual for the sisters to squabble this way.

'I don't even *want* to be like you,' said Rathna.

'What are you trying to say? That you're noble? That I'm mean?'

'You should think before you talk about things you know nothing about, Saroja. Who do you think a husband is? Do we need another God? The one who will stand by us in our troubles and joys is no one else but the husband. They are the ones who slog outside. If they lose their temper, it's for us to keep calm.'

'But don't you slog in the house?'

'Look, Saroja! Such talk sounds smart up to a certain age, not anymore. You're old enough to get married. Forget such big talk.'

'You call this big talk? Fine! If this is bragging, so let it be. I have a temper to match his.'

'I don't know how to argue with you. But just because you can beat me in bickering, it doesn't mean you've defeated me. I'm the kind who'll live my life according to the principles *I* believe in.'

Saroja had retaliated angrily, 'If I had been in your place, I would've hurled that plate back at him.'

She bit her tongue; she should not have said that. But the words had been spoken. A spoken word is like a broken pearl. Can you say you'll take it back and mend it?

As Rathna heard her sister speak that way, she burst out crying. Delving deep into her grief and talking about it incoherently, Rathna had gone to her bedroom. Her sobs could be heard beyond the closed door.

'What have I done?' thought Saroja, 'They're husband and wife. Whatever they may do to each other, why should I talk about it? They'll get together, anyway.'

But deep within her, Saroja knew Rathna was crying bitterly not because of what *she* had said. It was an ache of many days. Could it be that she had pin-pointed Rathna's inability to talk back to her husband? She could not show the pain she had felt at the violence with which the plate had been thrown at her. Could there be an obscure need to find some excuse to let that grief flow out of her? Could what she had said be only an excuse for her sister to weep for the disgust she had felt at her husband's behaviour? Such a quarrel between them was not anything new. Then, why had she not fought back as usual? Why did she have to weep so much this time?

Rathna had not come out of the bedroom the whole day. She did not even come out to eat. Saroja too had not eaten. Why should she eat if her sister did not? She had spent the day talking pointlessly to Ravi and feeding him something or the other; he had been calling for his mother, 'Amma, Amma.'

The door opened about ten or fifteen minutes before the husband was due to return. Rathna washed her face, put a kumkuma on her forehead, changed her sari and made herself presentable. Her face was blotched with weeping but her husband did not ask her why she looked that way. As soon as he came, he had a wash, came in and said, 'Is there any chick-pea flour in the house? Fry some bajjis with it.'

'He was born to eat,' mouthed Saroja's lips, out of ear-shot.

Rathna had rushed about and made the snack and served him. He had not even looked up at the face of the wife who stood near. He ate reading the paper. He burped. Because he had said, 'I don't want coffee,' tea was served. He drank it and went out. He returned home around nine. Dinner was ready by then. He ate and slept. 'Have you eaten? Have you been out?' No concern of that kind.

Except for the incident of the morning, the day had been like any other. But Saroja had been so shaken up that she could not sleep that night. She lay beside Ravi with her arm around him, eyes closed. She felt sick to hear Rathna's muted groans, the tinkle of her bangles, the creak of the cot. Realizing that Ravi too was born of such a union, she removed her arm and turned the other side; she did not want to have anything to do with him.

For the next two days, the sisters did not talk to each other. 'My brother-in-law keeps to himself anyway. But now my sister too. Why did I have to come at all?' Saroja felt her throat tighten. She could not decide to go home suddenly; that would be like the saying: one stroke, two pieces. Also, she would have to reply to everyone's, 'Why? Why?' She managed to stay on for a few days feeling, 'We're sisters, after all.' And then she left. 'I'm going. I'm bored here,' she had said.

Parthakka teased her, 'You'd said you'd go for a month. Why are you back so soon?' To which, Gowramma had added, 'Can she lord it over everyone there as she does here? She must've got bored. No wonder she's back.' Saroja stared at her mother. Did she have any inkling of her son-in-law's behaviour? But that smiling face did not give away anything. Perhaps behind that smile was the feeling, 'My responsibility towards one girl is over. When will it be done with the next one?' Nothing more.

The rift between the sisters closed eventually and they drew close again. But, from that day, Saroja would not go anywhere near her brother-in-law. She would not give him a tumbler of coffee even when someone asked her to. Rathna knew the reason and so she did not provoke her sister. What if the stink of her family life spread all over?

When Saroja heard that the time had come for Rathna to go back to her house she was in an inexpressible turmoil. She felt she had to talk to her sister about a few things. But, then Rathna might assert her elder-sister's status with, 'Who do you think *you* are to teach me such things?' After all, she was only a younger sister, wasn't she? Saroja was irked, 'Have I let myself be so helpless? Sitting about as if my hands are tied?'

Not that Saroja had ever thought she herself would not get married. All she desired was a life without such irritations; a life of harmony. By the time Rathnakka was as old as she, Saroja, was now, Ravi had already been born. But she, Saroja, was not even married yet. All her days were slipping away with her duties in the kitchen. Sometimes, she sat day-dreaming about the kind of man she would marry. If only she could find him she would marry him; whatever be his caste. She felt like telling her parents, 'If I don't find the man of my dreams, I won't get married to just anyone only so that you may be rid of your burden.' He should be good-looking. He must be intelligent. He must have a heart too. She would marry someone who would take her away from traditional beliefs about God and family, beliefs one cannot hold, one cannot shed. He should love their companionship; love their life together, respect it. Talking, eating, sleeping ... she should be able to enjoy all that; transcend all that and grow into a greater awareness of their togetherness ... with him....

She had believed she would marry such a person whatever be his caste. True. But if such a situation did, indeed arise, would she have the courage to act? Surely, her mind was not a nest for impotent fury and anxieties that could not be laid to rest?

She could not talk to her father about anything. As for Parthakka and Gowramma, let alone talking about marriage, she could not even utter the first syllable, *ma* of the word, maduve. They would only think, 'O, the girl is hankering after marriage.' But how could she bring her thoughts into the open if she did not open her mouth? She would not get a true picture of herself through merely letting her feelings ebb and flow within her. 'Will anyone come who will make me open my mouth? Will he know I'm waiting for him? ...'

As she let her thoughts meander, Saroja felt how lucky Bhaskaranna's wife was. The image of Bhaskara drifted before her eyes. Her heart ached that she had to think of Parthakka's son, Bhaskara, as Bhaskar*anna*. If only she could marry someone like him everything would be linked together to form one meaning—the wedding music, the mantras[1] that are chanted, the mantapa[2] in which the ceremony is performed, the dhaare;[3] the very ritual of giving away a daughter, why even the invitees, the wedding feast, the gifts. Everything would be strung together to form a necklace; they would not be separate items that go with a wedding. But had there ever been a wedding of that kind anywhere?

If she waited for a person of her choice, she might have to wait until her cheeks became sunken, her hair white, and her skin wrinkled. Saroja shuddered at the thought. But she also hoped she would not say 'yes' to anyone in sheer desperation. 'What if that person is also like Rathnakka's husband? Unresponsive to any of my feelings, not touching me in any way but one, won't he keep me as an untouchable? Won't he remain an untouchable to my dreams and fantasies? And will our children have untouchable minds unable to quiver with my dreams and aspirations?' Saroja sighed, deep in thought.

---

[1] mantras: vedic chants; power generated by the recitation of a word or words
[2] mantapa: dais on which the wedding ceremony is performed
[3] dhaare: ritual of giving away a daughter in marriage

seven

Sheena

In the month of Jyeshta,[1] Shreenivasa came home after his exams. His holidays coincided with the monsoon, right when his siblings had to get back to school after the summer break. All he did was talk of Bhaskara and his wife whom he had been visiting frequently. Bhaskara had asked him to call on them.

'Of course, he'll ask you! Did you think he wouldn't be upset about people *not* visiting him?' fumed Parthakka, 'If you ask me, Sheena, I think you should let him feel upset. It's wrong for you to go there.'

'I knew you'd say this. That's why I didn't make the mistake of asking you,' replied Sheena, his smile touching the tips of his moustache. 'What do *you* know, Parthakka? When you're away from home even the news of a wasp from your hometown visiting in the vicinity is a cause for great jubilation. Nothing you say will keep me from visiting them.'

To Sheena, Bhaskara's wife was a good woman. He called her athigay as if she were his sister-in-law. 'She didn't know a thing about cooking! Bhaskaranna had to teach her everything.'

'That's his karma.'

'What's this about fate, Parthakka?' Saroja butted in, 'Shouldn't men cook at all? You're being your own peevish self as usual. So pointless!'

---

[1] Jyeshta: onset of monsoon

'However much you may fly about, henne, it's in the kitchen you'll have to land, finally. If men were supposed to cook where was the need for women on earth? If the man has to teach his wife to cook, it's a sure sign that Kaliyuga is drawing to a close. What would that Korathi know? She may reheat stale cooked rice with some water. Perhaps the meat of buffalo, cow....'

'You shouldn't be saying such things, Parthakka,' Sheena stopped her. 'They cook our kind of food whenever I visit them. Bhaskaranna has even taught her to make pachadi with banana stem. His patience is Patience!'

'What's this, Sheena? Does it mean you've even eaten in her house? What's come over the two of you, father and son? Someone's cast a spell on you, I'm sure of it now! O God, can't you take me away quickly?' wailed Gowramma, wiping her eyes.

'Why do you say, *her* house, Amma? It's theirs. Say, *their* house,' Sheena corrected his mother, laughing.

'I don't need any dog to teach me. For someone who's eaten in a Koraga's house, you do have the audacity to correct *me*, don't you?' Gowramma, who could not speak out against her husband, lashed out at her son. 'We must have performed your upanayana because of some sin in some previous birth. We could've saved ourselves that expense by not doing it. It's as if we spent money to drive out Dharma from our house.'

Sheena became solemn, 'Amma, have you seen our college? Boys from different countries, belonging to different religions come to study there. Don't I eat with them? In the future, there might be a separate caste of people who keep harping on caste all the time. Most of the others won't care.'

Parthakka intruded as if something had flashed through her mind suddenly, 'Haan, is it true, mani? Is it true that you have to touch women during periods? Women who've just had babies? Dead bodies?'

'Yes.'

'You have a bath as soon as you return to your room, don't you?'

'There's an Ajji in our hostel, Parthakka. As soon as we return, she mixes cow dung in water and pours the slurry over our heads to purify us ... on all of us.'

'Aha, that's a lie!' remarked Shiva. When Shiva spoke as if it had struck him alone that Sheena was joking, all the others laughed. All except Parthakka and Gowramma, that is.

'Parthakka, haven't you anything better to worry about?' continued Sheena, 'Once we cross the threshold of our homes, who bothers about the madi that comes with pouring cow dung water on us? Okay, let that be. You talk so much. Do you know what periods is all about? Shall I tell you?'

'O, don't, maharaya! Why, is it my fate to hear about it from *your* mouth? Shee ... shee.... If you have to learn about such things, it must be *your* karma.'

'Whatever you say, Parthakka, as for me, all I want is cleanliness. Why do we talk of not eating food eaten by others? Why do we wash dishes after use? Isn't it because we want to be hygienic? Go and see Bhaskaranna's house. It sparkles like a mirror; it's that clean. And athige is warm and hospitable every time I visit them. Do you think she's happy being married to a Brahmin? Her own people have cast her out of the community. Not because she's married to a Brahmin. I heard they do it to anyone who marries someone from a different caste. Bhaskaranna isn't upset about it. He said he had expected it. "What's so surprising about it when people think caste is more important than being humane," he says.'

'Being humane? What was the great compassion he saw in her? Something he couldn't see among people of his own caste? Such respectable families came forward to give their girls to him. Why did he reject all of them? Is it because they weren't humane enough?

'About that, you'll have to ask your son. I don't know the answers. That's not what he's asking for either. All he wants to know is this: what's so inhuman in what they've done? For that matter, even athigay is equally strong-willed. She won't go where she's not accepted. "Who says we'll survive only if these people give us a caste?" she asks.'

'Look at that! Don't keep referring to her as athigay, athigay. Is she some special sister-in-law of yours? When will *you* see some sense? The flirt! She'll ask whatever she wants if she has people like you who'll listen.'

'Don't say such foul things, Parthakka. That's not true. Do you know how much she respects you? Bhaskaranna has told her everything about you, about how you brought him up through tough times. Everything. "Won't she ever come to live with us in our home?" she keeps asking with deep longing.'

'O, stop it, maga! This Parthakka doesn't belong to the type who'll be moved by such things. I have your Amma and Appa. They'll look after me when I'm too old to move about. I'm a widow with a shaven head. Why should *I* compromise my madi by going to *her* house? I'm not prepared to be thrown into some unseen hell. All of you are here. I think of you as my children. Will you abandon me?'

'Believe me, she grieves that she's separated a son from his mother.'

'Did she tell you that?'

'Does she have to tell me? I can make out from the way she talks.'

'You can make out! Nonsense! You think you can understand the universe because you've sprouted a moustache! Here, Gowri, I've lost the only son I had. Now, I'm afraid I'll make you lose your son too. Scold him. Screw his ears and make him see sense.'

'I'm not a little child for you to advise me. Okay, if it makes you happy to scold athigay, if you think that's the only way to make *me* understand, go ahead, scold her. Scold her with words that do or do not exist. But when I was ill, she was the one who looked after me, gave me the right diet. When Appayya delayed in sending me money, she's the one who lent it to me on her own. Of course, I returned it later but that's not the point. She gave it to me when I needed it! If she helped me out in my moment of need, doesn't it show her compassion? Bhaskaranna too is like her. One must learn from him how to look after a wife.'

'Enough, maharaya! Have they come down from heaven or what?'

'If you keep talking this way, what can I say? No, they don't look as if they've descended from heaven but, thank God, they haven't left the earth and flown away. Be thankful for that. Visit them once, Parthakka. Then you can talk.'

Gowramma glowered at him. 'Stop being impertinent, mani! Is that any way to talk to her?'

'I haven't asked for anything else in this life,' said Parthakka, 'I only hope God won't give me another birth.'

Her voice seemed to rise from somewhere deep inside her.

Ever since Sheena came home, the children felt they had grown new wings. Shiva pestered his elder brother to teach them a new play but Sheena was not enthusiastic about such things any more. At the most, he would sing for them.

'If it's to be a song, okay, sing a song. But you have to teach us too,' persisted the children. And so he taught them devotional songs. They sang Paahi Shantha Bhuvaneshwara to the Lord of the Earth asking Him to watch over them and Giridhara Brijadhara Murali Adharadhara to Krishna, who carries mountains; who lives in Brijabhumi; who plays the flute. They also sang a hymn in Marathi, 'Ugada Nayana Deva, open your eyes, O God' and another in Kannada to the son of Shiva and Parvathi, 'Gajavadhana Beduve, I plead with you, O Ganesha.'

Sheena joined them during the bhajane[2] in the evenings. When he said, 'Whether I have faith in God or not, I feel happy to sing these hymns and so I come for the bhajane,' the children stared at him wide-eyed not quite comprehending what he meant. When he closed his eyes and sang, a restrained solemn devotional like a devaranama[3] would become a bhavageethe, wrought with emotion. At times, Vasudevaraya would come in from the veranda to listen to him. Rathna too would come with the baby, to sit for a while leaning against a wall. Though her stomach was bound tightly with a sari, Parthakka insisted that Rathna had to sit against a wall; or else her back would become stiff and achy as she got older. Sometimes, the whole family gathered there and joined Sheena in the singing. At such times, Putta felt God manifesting Himself. He could see God even with his eyes closed. Blue Rama, Rama with His bow. Aapadaam apahartharam, the deliverer from all danger, Putta could lisp the whole song. He had told his friends that if anyone went to bed after reciting it, he could sleep soundly even after listening to a story about a demon. He had also told them he had stopped wetting his bed.

At the end of the bhajan, there was an arathi to the ten incarnations of Vishnu. Everyone received the arathi praising Krishna who blessed

---

[2] bhajane: devotional songs
[3] devaranama: hymn

Pundalika, namaha pundalika varadha ... and, as they prostrated before God, they ended their worship with sarvejanaah sukhino bhavanthu, praying that everyone may prosper and be happy.

Rathna had gone from this home. She loved to sing the evening bhajan and worship God this way in her husband's home too. But none of her neighbours did it and so she felt embarrassed to sing aloud.

'What kind of modesty is that?'

'What do you all know? Here, in this big house, no one hears you however loudly you scream. Is it the same there?'

'Yes, yes! What if she sings and the whole neighbourhood runs away from their homes?' teased Shiva.

'O, go on! I sing better than you, you know.'

'Does Sheena pray there? Here, he used to mutter a bit of the Gayathri Japa for fear of Parthakka,' wondered Gowramma, and turning to Sheena she said, 'Will you tell me now, mani? Where's your janivara? Show me, let me see it.'

'Ayyo, Amma, why do you bother me?' drawled Sheena, grimacing so dramatically that everyone, right down to Ravi, laughed out loud.

'What's the great bother? Didn't we spend so much to have a grand upanayana because you're our first-born?'

'Yes, that was the mistake. You should've waited until I turned eighteen. I'm not responsible for crimes committed when I was a minor.' Sheena looked at Shiva, raising his eyebrows as if to say, 'How d'you like my legal jargon?'

Anyway, in whatever way they led their individual lives, whenever they came home, all the children joined in singing the Bhajane and reciting the Japa. It was a rule that no plates would be set for dinner until a few hymns were sung and the arathi done. The evening worship started early so that supper could be on time. Parthakka, sitting in a corner, legs outstretched, managed a few catnaps while chanting the names of Rama. Sometimes, while she dozed, her head tilted backwards and her sari slipped, revealing her head. And Putta was not Putta if he did not notice the lolling bald head and stop his prayers midway to call out, 'Oi! How much do five seers of jaggery cost?' And that was enough; Parthakka would wake up, would even giggle sheepishly.

Trying to restrain his laughter, Putta would clap aloud and repeat after Sheena a song by Punrandaradasa: 'Beat your hand on the drum, khad, khad! Let your body be drunk with joy!' The other children too felt like clowning a bit, naturally.

There were times when Rathna's baby joined in the singing. But as she began her whine, the singers protested, 'Ei, Rathnakka, stop playing your harmonium and go out!'

eight

The Namakarana

At last, Rathna's husband arrived. As Sheena was home, he could keep him company. Rathna's husband wore such a grumpy expression that it could roast a single grain of paddy into a handful of puffed rice. But to nine words from Sheena, he added at least one to make conversation. As the son-in-law of the house, he was very decorous. He kept to the veranda; he was not the kind to wander freely about the house. Only once, as a matter of courtesy, he went to the young mother's bedroom and made a pretence of looking at his baby. He did not touch her even with the tip of a finger nail. Rathna's face opened out like a winnowing fan as soon as he entered. She told him about the baby's antics without his asking. He merely said, 'Hm ... mm,' in a dry voice and walked out, proving Parthakka right; one had to learn from him how to be dignified. He had brought his mother-in-law a sari with a grand jari border as a customary gift for having looked after his wife during childbirth and after. Gowramma received it with an embarrassed, 'You gave me one last time. Did you have to bring one again?' But not a single expression like, 'O, that doesn't matter,' slipped out of her mouth.

'That's so typical of him,' gushed Gowramma, 'For him, a tradition is meant to be honoured. He gives respect where respect is due. No one has to teach him such things. He doesn't even think of the expense.'

'That's very true!' Rathna had to add her bit, 'When it comes to reverence to elders, he becomes Sri Rama himself. Look at the saris he's bought me. See, how good they are! I don't have to worry about such things at all.' Saroja noticed that Rathnakka's statements had no connection with one another.

On the day of the namakarana, most of the guests were from his side. During previous occasions of festivity many more of the neighbouring families would have turned up but not this time because Parthakka was here. 'Just as well,' thought Rathna's parents. Her husband's family sat around Parthakka and got as much information as possible about Bhaskara. The more she told them, the more they wormed out of her. Spent, Parthakka went into the kitchen and did not come out again.

Rathna wanted a name with just two syllables for the baby but her husband named her Suguna.

'Did bhavayya name her the good-natured-one because he doesn't have that quality?' Saroja whispered in Sheena's ear.

The guests felt it was old-fashioned.

'They can call her Guna,' said someone.

'Thuuu, what kind of a name is that? It just means the nature of a person,' said another.

'She could be Suggi[1] too,' suggested Rathna's husband with a ghost of a smile flitting across his mouth.

'He does have a sense of humour, doesn't he? Shortening her name to mean harvest,' someone simpered with admiration. But he did not want any pet names for the baby; he wanted her to be called Suguna.

The chubby three-month old was happy with anyone. She danced about shaking her limbs until she was hungry. Rathna's husband had brought a gold necklace for his daughter. As it hung from her neck, some people lifted it in their hands to make out its weight. There were only earrings from her maternal grandfather. They had given her a pair of anklets already, hadn't they? When Ravi was born, they had given him a brass cradle and a gold necklace weighing two sovereigns because he was the firstborn.

Can we do that every time? We've other daughters too, don't we? We'll have to do the same for them as well. Can we treat them differently, giving more to one and less to the others? Was their argument.

---

[1] Suggi: harvest

Sheena, as the baby's maternal uncle, took his niece on his lap and the goldsmith pierced her ears and inserted tiny ear-rings. She screamed with shock and pain. Everyone felt sorry for her. The goldsmith was duly honoured with betel leaves and nuts, a coconut, a measure of rice, and some money.

'Her Ajja could've got a pair for gold bangles made for the baby,' whispered Rathna's husband in her ear, 'I haven't compromised on the traditional practices in any way. Then why does he belittle me in front of others?'

Rathna did not speak a word. Even she felt, 'Yes, Appayya could've given the baby a pair of bangles. Was Saroja's wedding fixed for him to worry of that expense? This was the only expense for now, wasn't it? At least Amma should've told Appayya about it.'

As if by magic, Narpate[2] and her friends appeared at the garbage dump in a corner of the backyard during lunch. Despite their protests, the guests had been served a lot more than they could eat. And so the banana leaves that were thrown on the garbage had heaps of leftover food. The Koraga women fell upon it with great relish, all the while trying to push away dogs and crows that also crowded round the leftovers.

Putta was playing marbles in the yard with his friends who had come for the namakarana. He was stunned to see the crowd near the dump. He stopped playing and ran over to them.

'Narpate! What? You are eating here?' he asked, shocked.

'Yes, channodayare! What a tasty food!'

'But don't eat it. Thuuu, it's enjalu! People have eaten it. It's leftover food!'

Narpate laughed out aloud. The other women joined her. As they continued eating, Putta said again, 'We shouldn't eat enjalu. Doesn't Parthakka say so? Don't eat it.'

'Go, odeyare, go and play.'

The Koraga women carried on eating, laughing, and talking among themselves. Putta could not understand a single word. He was upset.

'I must go and tell Parthakka,' he thought to himself, 'She won't let them eat this. She'll give it to them. *"Don't* step into our yard again,"

---

[2] Narpate: a woman who has nothing to call her own; an outcaste

she'll say.' He went looking for Parthakka and found her in the kitchen where festive cooking was usually done. She was seeing to the cooking vessels being washed and stacked.

'Parthakka! Parthakka!'

'Don't call me, mani. I'm busy right now,' she said, gently.

'Come here for just a minute,' said Putta, going towards her.

'Will you get out or not?' she shouted.

Putta walked away, crestfallen. He told his friends about Narpate and her friends.

'They come to our houses too,' they said. 'They come whenever we have a feast and they crowd round the garbage heap and eat the leftovers.'

'Oho! So that's how it is, is it?' thought Putta, 'They're doing the same here.'

The Korathis ate with greater excitement than the guests. They ate as much as they could and wrapped up the leftovers in areca sheaths and took it home.

The next day, Putta, Jaya, and Shami threw a tantrum. They did not want to go to school as Rathna was leaving by the eight o'clock bus. But their ploy did not work for they could see her off and then go to school. Gowramma went with the mother and child as previously planned. Rathna wept like a child as she prostrated before the family gods, her parents, and Parthakka. Vasudevaraya too swallowed thrice to control his grief.

'I don't know how the days went by. How will we live now?' fretted Parthakka. 'Come here, mani,' she called Ravi and pressed a ten-rupee note into his palm, 'Don't trouble your mother. Be obedient, maga. Give the money to your mother. Don't lose it. Don't spend it. Save it in a dumb-box.' Ravi nodded as if he understood what she was saying. He was happy to be holding the money. Rathna's husband was already near the auto-rickshaw. Seeing him looking elsewhere and smoking a cigarette, Saroja hissed like water on ember, 'Sheenanna, look at that dour bag of tamarind! *Sthitha prajnasya kaa bhasha....* He does look like an embodiment of poise, doesn't he?'

Sheena, who had kept his Bhavayya company the last few days agreed in a low voice. Shiva was curious about their whisperings but did not have the patience to find out what it was all about. He watched the ritual of farewell with interest as if it were a play. Jaya and Shami hugged and kissed the baby many times under the pretext of bidding her goodbye. She seemed to enjoy the attention; not a whimper from her. In fact, she was livelier than ever. Rathna looked back at her family over and over again until her husband said impatiently, 'Hm, enough! Get in, get in!' and she got into the autorickshaw. Gowramma got in right behind her, carrying the baby. Rathna's husband pressed his palms together to bid goodbye to his father-in-law and shook hands with Sheena. And the auto went away. The children kept waving until it sped out of sight.

Parthakka became moody after Rathna left. She sat brooding, 'Rathna left towards the end of Jyeshta. Now Ashaada is over and Shravana has begun. The baby will start teething in another month. Then she'll have loose motions. She will have to be looked after carefully. Had she been here, I would've put her on my legs and pressed a pod of garlic on to her palate to keep the soft-spot on the head from sinking. Then the watery stools will stop. I wonder how Rathna will manage there. Gowri had said I could stay with Rathna for a few months to help her out. But I don't feel up to it, somehow. I don't feel like going out of this house to anyone else's door even for a day. Why should I go? Wherever I may go, the first four days may be fine but the fifth day won't. Only here I'm not an outsider. Vastheva hasn't denied me anything; neither love nor trust. He respects me as an elder. He collects the five measures of rice due to me from my father-in-law's household as ashanaartha for my upkeep. I don't have to worry about anything. If there's any place I should go to at all, there's only one. That's Bhaskara's house. That was my dream house, but my dream of bringing him up to brighten my old age was a waste. What's in our hands? Nothing at all except the illusion that *I* can do something or that I've *done* something. The planning is ours, the decision is Brahma's. Nevertheless, being born as human beings, we do have desires, don't we? I want to stretch my legs this way and sit in my son's house for a few days. These hands have bathed, rocked to sleep, and fed ganji to so many babies. They've pressed pods of garlic to the palate, ground medicinal herbs and tended them. Now the longing to do the same for my grandbaby wells up from deep inside me. But I have only to think of that thoti woman and the desire dies as if it had never been. I've opened out my heart to Gowri hoping to lessen the heat of the rage in my belly. But the fire seems never to die down though it does abate for a while.'

Gowramma had no time to listen to Parthakka, anyway. If she had one family in the house, she had another in the cowshed. They had only to hear her lift the latch early in the morning to start mooing, 'Ambaa!' She scolded them gently, lovingly, 'What now? Am I to bring you your feed as soon as I open my eyes?' Though she talked to them as if they could understand, they did not stop saying, 'Ambaa, ambaa.' Gowramma went straight to the parapet in the cowshed. The three cows and even the lazy buffalo rested their heads on the low wall as if to say, 'Come on! Feed us.' 'O! As if I've nothing else to do as soon as I wake up every morning,' she said, petting them, caressing their forehead and the lose skin hanging under the neck. They never had enough of it; each one tossed its head where it was tethered wanting to be the one to be petted. 'This is a bonding, isn't it? Who are they and who am I? And yet, is their love any less than anyone else's?' mused Gowramma as she stood awhile mumbling sweet nothings to them.

Then, returning to the courtyard, she plucked a mango leaf, rolled it and brushed her teeth with it, cleaned her tongue with the midrib and washed her face. She went inside to comb her hair and stick a few flowers in it before she lit the oven in the kitchen for coffee and the one in the bathroom for bathwater and another for cattle feed on which rice gruel had been made for them in the previous night. By the time she put out the dirty pots and pans, the water for coffee came to a boil. Adding coffee powder to it and letting it brew, she mixed feed for her children in the cowshed—warm gruel, oil cakes, ground cotton seeds, and some salt—and poured it into their buckets, as much as each would eat. They enjoyed their breakfast, chomping and slurping. Even as Saroja milked them and came into the kitchen to see to the gruel for the family, Parthakka put out some bundles of grass. From then until around ten o'clock when Rukku gave them oil cakes in water and the cowherd drove them out to graze, they could keep calling, 'Ambaa, ambaa'; they would not get anything else.

Then started the day's cooking for the family with morning coffee, the raw rice gruel for breakfast, lunch, and coffee again with snacks for tea-time ... the chores chased each other endlessly throughout the day, every day.

Despite the daily grind, the Karkataka Sankramana or the first day of Shravana[3] brought great excitement to Gowramma. She never failed to adorn the threshold with flowers throughout the month. Of course, she had the daily habit of drawing parallel rangoli lines across it soon after her bath. Only then did she have her coffee. But this excitement was different. A lot of preparation went into worshipping the hosilajji,[4] the granny of the threshold, during Shravana. Five or six days before the beginning of the month, Gowramma soaked some ragi and horse gram and sowed them on a spread of mud, covering the spot with used biscuit tins or mud pots. What an air of expectancy as she gently lifted the tin covers on the shankranthi of Shravana! The children gathered round her and gasped with joy as she displayed a rich growth of fresh seedlings; delicate silk-soft stems holding aloft tuft-like yellow flowers. Locally, the flowers were called kollu-hoovu and were traditionally considered auspicious for worshipping the threshold. Shaavige[5] had to be cooked that day to bind the hosilajji to the house symbolically with strands of the vermicelli. Together with shaavige, modaks made of wheat flour had to be offered to the Gods as naivedya.[6] It was customary to bind the hosilajji on Simha Sankramana and to release her on the following Simha Sankramana. So dosay had to be made for the next Sankramana. Shami and Jaya gathered flowers from the garden and ferns called crow-feet and sparrow-feet that had sprouted on the garden walls, thanks to the monsoon rains. They too drew rangoli lines on thresholds with great enthusiasm on the Simha Sankramana.

'Houses don't have thresholds these days. Bald, bare houses! What kind of a home is a house without the naivedya and puje for the

---

[3] Shravana: month during which the threshold is worshipped.
[4] hosilajji: the threshold-granny
[5] shaavige: vermicelli
[6] naivedya: food offered to the Gods

hosilu?[7] A house without domesticity!' said Gowramma to Parthakka as she got things ready for the puje. By the time she drew the rangoli lines on the threshold, adorned it with some flowers, smeared some turmeric and kumkuma on it, broke a coconut and completed the puje by offering it bananas and the naivedya of shaavige and modak, Gowramma was wet with perspiration.

For the whole month, whatever be the special dish, hosilajji had to get the first share. Using her as a pretext, the family feasted on such delicacies as dosay, kadabu, pathroday every Tuesday and Friday throughout the month. One of them would tease, 'Ai, be careful! Hosilajji may have a stomach upset if she eats so much!' Every evening, as soon as the lamps were lit, Gowramma lit a lamp at the threshold, prostrated before it, adorned it with a few sanje mallige, offered a naivedya of sugar in milk and stuck the flowers in her hair. Her daughters prostrated after her. Only Putta got to drink the naivedya. After that, she placed the lamp in front of the gods and each of them went round and round thrice in the same spot before prostrating before God.

'Have you lost your senses to gyrate that way?' teased Shiva. The girls giggled helplessly.

'Why, mani? Have *you* lost yours? You're not letting us worship!' Gowramma scolded him as she prostrated before God and went about her work.

Once in a way, some Konkani women like Sanjeevi or Shanthi came by to pick rathnagandhi and hibiscus from her garden, make choodies[8] and ask Gowramma to decorate her threshold with the posies.

No one knew how the month slipped by, what with the feasting on special snacks, all in Hosilajji's name.

---

[7] hosilu: threshold
[8] choodies: small posies of flowers

nine

The Koosa Woman

'Odathiyaraa!'

That was the Koosa woman calling the women of the household. She usually brought grass for the cows. Gowramma was not the kind to come out at the first call. After letting her call out a few more times, she emerged with a, 'What now? What have you brought for your mistresses?' Chathurthi of Bhadrapada[1] was two days away bringing with it the Ganesha festival and the woman had brought a bundle of munduga leaves. She put it down in the yard at a distance and stood waiting without removing the coil of cloth on her head. She was heavily pregnant.

'How thorny the leaves are, Amma! I have scratches all over. We don't get these anywhere around here these days. I had to go far for it ... very far. Anyway, I was able to bring you at least this much.' Every word hinted that Gowramma should pay her a little more than she intended to. Gowramma took out an eight-anna bit from the banana-like bump she had made in her sari to tuck in the pleats at the waist and threw it into the out-stretched palm. Koosa took the coil of cloth from her head and sat down.

'Why've you sat down? I've got work to do inside. Go home now.'

'I was going home anyway. But what have I to do there, Amma? There's not a grain of rice in the house. Hegde won't give us anything

---

[1] Bhadrapada: month during which the Ganesha festival is celebrated.

without payment. He gives rice and such things on credit only to those who have money. In fact, it's the wealthy ones who don't pay him what they owe. These eight annas will get me some salt, red chillies, and tamarind. What can we eat, Amma?' Koosa sat in the shade of a tree and poured out her woes.

Gowramma felt sad for her, 'What troubles these people have to face!' But all she said was, 'With all this, why do you keep bearing children? Can't you be a little careful?'

'Why worry about the children, Amma? God gives; God looks after them. What can we do for them, anyway? All we do is add a little more water to the gruel and share it among all of us.' That was what she always said. 'Odathi, the day's almost done. The children are waiting at home. If you can give me something....'

'Wait,' said Gowramma as she went in. Coming out with a measure of broken rice, she handed it to her with, 'Here, make some gruel for the children. *We* do as much as we can but *you*'re not trustworthy. You've been giving us less grass these days. When I watch you, you give us a fair quantity. When I don't, you give us less. As for the doray grass for the cows, you've not been giving more than two handfuls.'

'What can I do, you tell me, odathi? From where do you want me to get doray grass? There's no use telling you how difficult it is. I bring as much as I can get. I swear on my life.' Gowramma was not moved.

'You look as if your baby's due any time now? Yes?'

'Yes, odathi. But for the ten days I'll be in bed after the baby comes, my eldest daughter will bring you the bundles. You don't have to worry about the grass.'

She did not stir even after the conversation was over. Gowramma turned to go inside thinking, 'If she wants to sit, let her sit.'

'Odhathiyare, I don't have anything to wrap around me after the baby is born. If you could me give a length of cloth....' The Koosa woman asked hesitantly.

'O, you and your unending demands! I'll look for it tomorrow or the day after. I don't have the time now. Go!'

'Yes, odathi, yes, I'll go!' The woman looked happy as she walked away.

Though as black as coal, she was an attractive woman with her curly hair and a large kumkuma on her forehead. Nobody could say she had borne so many children.

Sometimes seeing someone decked up in gold, Parthakka would say, 'That Koosa who gets us grass would look much better in such finery than this woman.' She referred to her as if she had no name.

And if anyone asked her, 'Would *you* accept her dressing this way?' she would retort, 'Don't ask such stupid questions.'

The Koosa did not send her children to school. Her master had threatened to tie her to a pole in his yard and thrash her. Her master was the landlord from whose fields she cut grass that she sold to make a living. But with a lot of pleading she had got permission to send the youngest son. 'But he's no good, Amma,' she would say, 'He's only fit to roam the streets and eat snacks sold by the road-side. If he goes to school for four days, he stays away for eight. It's not as if he's all that worthless, though. He's very good at grazing cattle. Not one cow wanders away. Not one buffalo strays into other people's fields. These days you can earn Rs 10 a month for grazing a buffalo and Rs 7 for a cow, can't you? If he can graze cattle from four houses, he can make a living. Anyway, why does he need school? Does he have to open an office after his studies? Say he does open one and I visit him there, what if he says like my brother did, "*Ei*, who're you? Why have you come here?" And what if he marries a woman from the Battada Koosa sub-caste like my brother? In our community, aren't we superior to them? Then, it's all over with me, isn't it? That's why God said education is not for us, Amma. He knows this is what we'll do if we're educated.' When the Koosa spoke that way, Parthakka was amazed at her wisdom. She would even say, 'No one is as wise as that Koosa. Yes, people *should* stay where they belong. They should also *know* that they should stay just there. There was a time when people knew. Those were good times too. Things were cheap. Life has become difficult ever since Shudras learnt to stand up and speak for themselves. The cost of living has been rising. No one can afford to eat well these days. Everything is scarce. If we trample on Dharma, won't Dharma trample on us and kill us?' Parthakka did not need anyone to listen to her as she rambled on. The pillar in the veranda was good enough. Even the wall that she leant against was good enough.

Rukku poured water from a decent height over the munduga leaves to cleanse them ritually. Parthakka removed the thorns from the back and sides of the leaves, withered them slightly over burning paddy straw, coiled them and kept them aside. The next day, she uncoiled the limp leaves, sewed them up with bits of the midrib of coconut palms and shaped them like tall glasses to be used as moulds to make kadabus for Ganesha. Her thoughts strayed naturally towards Bhaskara: That boy had an extra stomach when it came to eating this local specialty; kadabus made in the mould of munduga leaves. Whenever she sat down to pin the leaves into shape, he would ask, 'What, Amma? Are you pinning leaves?' And if she replied absent-mindedly, '*Huun*,' he would say, 'Oho! So when did *you* become pinning leaves, Amma?' and laugh, happy to have caught her off-guard. It was a worn-out joke passed from mouth to mouth; 'pinning' was changed from a doing-word to a descriptive-word. But somehow it made her laugh whenever Bhaskara said it. Perhaps, it was the way he said it.

Parthakka became depressed. 'Wonder how he'll spend Ganesha Chathurthi there. Will that Korathi be able to make kadabus for him? Where do I have the good fortune to see my daughter-in-law cook for my son?'

The day before Chathurthi, Parthakka made kadabus with five seers of coarsely ground rice flour. She soaked two and half seers of black gram to mix with it and ground the soaked gram like one possessed though Saroja offered to help. But, the next day, those kadabus would not go down her throat though they were as soft and fluffy as cotton.

As they did every year this year too vatus[2] from the homes of purohits came throughout the day; smart little Brahmin boys coming for dhakshine. As soon as they entered the house, whoever was around gave each of them a few coins from the small change stored in a cup on a table for that purpose. The money was never more than two, four, or eight annas. In the evening, the Koragas came in groups beating their drums. To the high-pitched wailing of a single note from a flute and

---

[2] vatu: Brahmin boy

the heart-stopping dhad, dhad of the drum, they added their shouts of 'Kooo!' and 'O!' and jumped up to the rhythm as high as they could as if possessed. From every house they went to, they received an inferior variety of kadabus made for them with a batter of boiled rice and a smaller quantity of black gram set in cups made with jackfruit leaves. It was off-white in colour and hard. The leader of each group got one to be shared among its members. Who knew how many kadabus were steamed that day? Who could keep count?

Thinking of Bhaskara and his love for her kadabus, Parthakka could not eat a single bite the whole day. And seeing the troupes of Koraga dancers at Vasudevaraya's house that evening, she felt she was dying. Her whole being revolted at the sight. 'Abah! How very dark they were! What nakedness, what scanty clothing, and what a stench of liquor! And the screech of their flute and the thuds of their drum! Thuth! May a pit be dug and they be buried in it! And to think that a girl from such a herd is my sosay! Couldn't Bhaskara find anyone else?' As if the heart-ache was not hurting enough, when one of the groups came round, Rukku giggled saying, 'There! Some people from Parthakka's family have come!'

Parthakka could not open out the grief in her belly to Saroja. She was not like Rathna; neither as understanding nor as patient. How much could she tell Gowri or Vasudevaraya? The more she thought of it, the more she felt a fury rage within her, 'What a son! He's made it impossible for me to hold up my head in front of four people. He set out to redeem the country. He's ended up redeeming the mother who begot him. Serves him right! This is his fate. That girl has grown up eating hard bits of dirty-white kadabu begged from houses like ours. What kind of a Ganesha festivity would *she* be capable of? Anyway, whether she celebrates Ganesha or she doesn't, whether he eats kadabu or he doesn't, why should *I* wilt with hunger remembering that shameless son of mine?' That night, Parthakka forced down the kadabu with a little coconut oil, the gravy of some pickle, and three glasses of water. Only her tears flowed freely, unbidden.

Thoughts of Bhaskara kept needling her even as she lay down that night, 'How long is it since he got married? He should've had at least two children by now, shouldn't he? He hasn't had even one yet. Surely,

Vastheva would've told me if he had, wouldn't he?' Parthakka wished she could advice her son: 'Mani, is it enough to get married? You must have at least four children one after the other. The four children must be of four different kinds of temperament. Among them, one should be like you. Then you may open your eyes to the world. He should go about in the way you totally disapprove. Then you may understand my heart-ache.' But of what use would that be? Is he not the kind who will sew his lips together to keep them shut? Or, he might even say, 'Is that why you wish I had children, Amma? What kind of a blessing is that? I don't want *any* children.' But then, she could retaliate, 'Ahaha! Don't think it's that easy, mani. Are you a sanyasi[3] to say you don't want any children? Have you renounced the world? Isn't it said that even sages forget to chant their prayers when they hear a baby's cry? Wasn't an ascetic like Kanvarishi overcome with paternal love when he saw the baby Shakuntala? Didn't he bring her to his hermitage? If the man who believed he had given up the maya[4] of this world could bring her up like his daughter, it shows he was still trapped in the web of illusion. If not, he shouldn't have felt any grief in sending her away to her husband's house. But he did! Will I ever believe that the desires of the world that did not leave the rishis will let you be? Who else knows the depth of your mind as well as I do? But even then, I didn't expect you to do *this* to me some day. *That* was the illusion that trapped me; the illusion that there's nothing I don't know. I thought I knew you. Wasn't it only after you got married that I realized how little?'

Even as she carried on an imaginary dialogue with the son, she wondered, 'I think of my son all the time but does he ever think of me? I'd never let him eat as much as he wanted; I'd always make him eat until *I* was satisfied. How often has he said, "Don't serve me, Maharayithi. You serve me too much!" Who could talk like him? And whenever I made kadabu with munduga leaves, was he satisfied with mere chutney to go with it? After all, we were just the two of us, he and I, and yet he'd want every single dish that was supposed to be eaten with it—coconut chutney, a vegetable curry, a gravy with tamarind, the gravy of mango

[3] sanyasi: renunciate
[4] maya: illusion

pickle, and chillies soaked in curds, dried and fried, with ghee or coconut oil. And did I ever shirk work saying, "Why do I have to make all that for just the two of us, mani?" Didn't I also yearn to make everything my son loved to eat as long as I was strong enough to make them? And now such a boy has found even a Koraga woman tasty. Why hasn't my heart split in two yet?'

'Come to think of it, those were happy days. Bhaskara would eat whatever I made for him. He would go to school. "I'll study well and get a good job," he'd say, "and then see how I'll look after you." He said that, didn't he? What does it matter whether he did as he said or not. The boy did say that. That's enough for me.' Parthakka tried to find comfort in what her son had intended to do.

But why do I grieve now that he isn't looking after me? Doesn't it imply that the joy I felt then at what he said was only an illusion? But it didn't seem like an illusion when I felt it. And this grief isn't an illusion either. That was as real then as this is real now. Perhaps there isn't anything like absolute truth. It's only what we think it is; that's all. Even Bhaskara would've said the same thing. He was a great one for talking. How often he had laughed at my feelings about madi and mylige! 'It's enough if *you're* clean, Amma,' he'd say, 'With all this fuss about ritual purity and pollution, you'll never get moksha. For one thing, moksha is insipid. No one should try to reach it. If you do attain moksha, doesn't it mean you'll never be born again, Amma? That should never happen. Won't the world be barren without a mother like you?' He would carry on like this endlessly, seated by the oven or the grinding stone while I cooked.

'How he changed once he left the town for his studies! I never heard that kind of chatter, laughter, or teasing from him ever again. All he did was think and think. He would either read or think with his chin resting on the palm of his hand. And if I asked, "Mani, what's come over you?" he'd reply, "You won't understand, Amma."'

In a sense, he didn't deceive me at all. He always had compassion for Shudras, didn't he? That was the one issue over which we'd always quarrel. Right then I should've guessed he'd turn out this way. But I wasn't so perceptive. *I'*d feel like vomiting just to think of those people who pretended to bathe once in eight days, who'd eat anything, except snakes perhaps. But *he* wasn't like that. He'd go to their slums, he'd eat with them. They too were like that with him. They'd give their lives for him. But why? Because he'd do whatever they asked him to, that's why. If he hadn't, perhaps they'd have punched him in the face and beaten him up. There's no caste as bad as the Shudra. How many times I've told him, 'Look, maga, you don't have to worry about their condition. It's the burden of their birth. Whatever good you may do is only momentary.' But did he ever listen? 'What do you know, Amma?' he'd say, 'For thousands of years, no one has shown them any love. No one has asked them to come near them. Everyone has said, I'm different, you're different; I'm the wolf, you're the sheep. They too believed what we've told them. It has never occurred to them that they could also become wolves or tigers or lions. It hasn't occurred to them because their minds are blinkered; they've been made to believe they exist only to serve us. Isn't that true? Then, what right do we have to say they have no gratitude, no sense of obligation? Let them punch me, Amma, let them rip me up and hang me up as thorana[5] decorating the lintels of their homes. Maybe then I'll find my peace. Maybe then our crime would've received at least one thousandth part of the punishment it deserves.'

Bhaskara was always a little hot-headed. Why only Bhaskara? Wasn't his father too like him? How much he's harassed me! He'd have them come right into the house with his, 'Poor Shudras, poor people.' Which household did such things? No wonder people passed sarcastic comments wherever I went. Let alone purohits, even cooks thought twice about coming home for a shraddha or any other ritual. Was it right for them to cook in a house to which Shudras had free access? But those days are over. His days were done; he got up and left. What else will happen to a man who desecrates his dharma? He'll have to leave life midway and go.

'I tremble at such thoughts. Mani, if your Appa let them drink water in our home, you've taken one of their kind into the mantapa with you. Who can say what could happen at any given moment? Don't you want to live your whole span of life?'

Parthakka could not sleep. She had not rested even after lunch. Her thoughts had kept tumbling out relentlessly, one after the other.

[5] thorana: festoons on the main door

Vasudevaraya read out to her bits of information about Bhaskara from Sheena's letters: Bhaskaranna is hardly at home these days. He keeps travelling. He doesn't even say where he's going. He's gone down a bit. Though Athigay's very worried about him, he does whatever he pleases. He doesn't eat at mealtimes....

Pulling out a strip from the mat under her bed, Parthakka shredded it to bits as she asked herself questions for which she could find no answers,

Isn't this my karma? When *her* people too did not want this marriage, where was the need for him to take on the burden? Why should they be angry with him, anyway? Is it because he snatched away a girl from their herd? Why! Is she a celestial nymph, a Rambhe, or an Urvashi descended from heaven? They may not have even heard those names. Wonder how she looks? Why should I wonder? Don't I see them everywhere? Until now, I thought of them as those Koragas. Now all that's left is for me to think of them as my sosay's people. No one else goes around as well decked as these Koosa, Koraga women. With clips in their hair and saris neatly pleated, they don't care whether the style suits them or not. All they want is to imitate the upper castes; they have no identity of their own. And these days, they even have upper-caste names, names their tongues can't mouth correctly. Such tongue-twisters! Was it for nothing that the elders had predicted such things would happen towards the end of Kaliyuga?

By the time Parthakka felt drowsy mulling over these things, Koggappa Shetty's rooster crowed.

The next morning, even before she got down to work, Rukku broke the news, 'That Koosa woman died.'

'What? What are you saying?' cried Gowramma.

'Why? Am I so stupid as to lie to you, Amma?'

Hearing the news, everyone came outside, Parthakka, Saroja, and the younger ones.

'She was carrying twins; both of them were big. I wonder what that woman got to eat. People who can afford to eat well have babies like mice and people who have nothing to eat have babies they can't deliver. What do you say to this, Amma?'

'Stop talking nonsense and tell us what happened.'

'Is there any use in talking about what happened? After the babies came out of the Koosa so did bucketsful of blood. When they took her to a hospital in that condition, no doctor attended to her. By the time a midbai came, everything was over.' Rukku did not sound sad. In fact, she spoke as if she would have been surprised if it had *not* happened the way it did. Gowramma was thoughtful; she was used to seeing such things. Saroja sat down, shocked. Only Shiva spoke, 'Why didn't the doctor see her? Isn't he a doctor in a free-hospital? He has to see every patient who goes there. Or else, he can be sued.' Shiva was furious.

'Shivayya, that's what *you* say,' drawled Rukku, 'But have you ever seen someone going to a hospital without any money and returning alive? How can you go to court against him? Which fatherless lawyer will take up her case?' And added after a while, 'That doctor is an orthodox Brahmin, very particular about rituals; he gets up early to say the Gayathri Japa or do the Vedaparayana. And after all, this woman is a Koosa. Will he touch her? ... But, of course, when night comes, even the Korathi sweeper in the hospital will do for him.'

Parthakka was upset. She felt, 'Rukku has aimed that final sting at me, that's for sure. Where's the need for all this discussion over the death of a Koosa, anyway. The more we try to shut her up, the more Rukku will say something she shouldn't, just to spite me.' In a bid to curb the trend of the conversation, she said, 'Brahma had written on that Koosa's forehead that this was the way she had to die. Once He has written, do you think she would've lived even if the doctor had attended to her on time?'

'Then, obviously Brahma doesn't believe in madi if He writes on a Koosa's forehead too,' said Shiva but his words were destined to be heard and yet not heard in the great silence that enshrouded them.

Gowramma stepped out of her reverie. 'Right until last evening she was here, bringing us bundles of grass. I can't believe she's no more. She's been giving us grass for quite some years now.... It was her karma to work till the very end. *Paapa!* The last thing she'd asked me for was a strip of an old sari to cover herself. If only I'd given it to her! *Che*, I can't believe she's gone.' And after yet a while she said to Rukku, 'Enough of standing like a pillar. You've given us the news. Now, take care of the pots and pans. None of them are washed yet.'

And she went indoors.

The momentary shroud of sadness lifted and all the rest followed her into the house to see to what had to be done. Putta had to memorize the poem, *Jai, Bharat Mata ki!*[6] But his head was full of the Koosa's death. All he could understand was that the woman was dead. He needed to find out the details. Going over to Rukku, he asked, 'How did that Koosa die? What happened? Tell me all over again.'

'O, nothing much happened, ayya. There are not enough people in Japan to pack match-boxes. And so the Koosa's gone there,' said Rukku laughing, as she tucked up her sari to do the dishes.

Putta leaned against a pillar, sucking his thumb. Saroja had to go right up to him and take him indoors.

---

[6] Jai, Bharat Mata ki: Victory to Mother India! There is irony here. What kind of a victory is it for the country when a Koosa patient died because a Brahmin doctor would not treat her?

ten

Vasudevaraya

Just lately, Vasudevaraya too had been worried about Bhaskara. 'He's resigned after a difference of opinion with someone about something,' Sheena had written, 'They're running the house with his wife's earnings. He's hardly ever at home. Athigay's pregnant ...' At least they were getting some information as Sheena was in the same town. Vasudevaraya was not sure if he should tell Parthakka about her son. She was getting on in years. It would not be fair to tell her and upset her, but wouldn't it be wrong to *not* tell her? In his bid to uplift the lower castes Bhaskara had gone as far as to incite the Koosas to fight for their rights. The commotion had made headlines in the newspapers. Sheena also said the elders of the town had been keeping a tab on him since then.

'Bhaskara isn't doing anything wrong, true,' mused Vasudevaraya, That's why I made Parthakka welcome despite what people said, including my relatives. When I was younger I was the one who went about the streets during the Freedom Movement shouting, 'Swatantrya! Swatantrya!' I went to prabhat bheri early every morning to march to martial tunes like, Kadam Kadam badaaaye ja...! I've pulled down a few telegraph poles proclaiming, 'Jai, Bharat Mata ki!' And after we got Independence I was the one who made speeches at public functions: 'We've done great wrong. We've said to the Shudras that only *we* are the children of Bharat Mata; that *they* are to live here in our motherland only to serve us as slaves. We've kept them apart from us all these years even after we've gained our Independence. The stain of this sin can never be washed away....'

'Yet, I'm not completely free; I can't get rid of my prejudices. I don't know if it's the ambience in which I grew up or the age-old beliefs that are etched on my mind. I may sit beside a Shudra officer during a public meeting but I cannot sit beside him in my dining room and share a meal. That's impossible. And so I was amazed at Bhaskara's courage. When he got married to a thoti—of course, she's a bit educated—I looked deep into myself to see if my surprise had turned to joy but my conscience told me it hadn't. Somehow, even now I feel he shouldn't have done such a thing. But there's no point in keeping my distance with her. Sheena says, if they keep themselves clean, they're just like us, Appayya. You'll be surprised to see how athigay runs her home. If you visit Subramanya, for instance, you'll get an idea of the money he's made as a hotelier. There's no dearth of anything in his bungalow. And yet you should see the way he's kept it. His wife always looks as if she's just got out of bed. Subramanya's only pleasure in life is slogging, nothing else.

'And when I said to my son, "That's all very well, Maharaya, Bhaskara did what he did because he has the guts to digest the consequences of his actions. Don't *you* go and do anything like that now." Sheena said, "Appayya, I don't think I have Bhaskaranna's courage; not in *this* janma. But if I do get it at least in my next life, I'll be very happy." Wasn't I relieved to hear him say that? But I *did* visit them twice, didn't I? I didn't bother about any criticism or comment.'

The thought brought a little puff of self-esteem.

'There's no guile in that girl. She's been cast out by her family. She's happy to welcome anyone who visits their home. The first time I went there, I remember I had only a glass of milk and some fruits. But the very next day I was ashamed of myself. I went again and had lunch with them. That was the charm of her hospitality. And how I enjoyed that meal! Real Kota Brahmin cooking! Bhaskara's training, of course! He has a flair for cooking. That boy learnt to cook sitting by his mother in the kitchen and talking his head off while she cooked. Once when Parthakka was down with fever, he had cooked some special dishes and invited his friends to show them off. Won't he train his wife now? Even her gojju[1] made with black gram flour was delicious. It smelt so good too. She had ground red chillies, mustard, and coconut and added it to the vegetable dish. And she's quite good-looking too. As Sheena said, if there's a system in their lives, you can't make out the difference between them and us. Of course, she's very dark but there's a certain charm about her—a liveliness. Would she have been worthy of our Bhaskara's hand if she hadn't been so attractive?

'Arare! Look at the way I'm thinking. Look at the way my bias has sneaked out from behind a veil to suggest that Bhaskara's superior to her. Why shouldn't I think *Bhaskara's* got a fine girl? Why didn't I think the culture she's been bred in has some value too? Why am I trying to find comfort in seeing her as one of *us*, seeing her cooking as being like *ours*? But why am I talking about myself? What about Bhaskara's attitude? The way he's been training her to be like us shows that *he's* also thinking like me without being aware of it, doesn't it?

'I don't think we can be rid of these prejudices so soon, so easily. These convictions live in the recesses of our minds, spinning cobwebs to trap us. They creep up on us and devour us when we least expect them. But will a lifetime do to sweep them away? God alone knows how many times we have to be born again and again. Our rebirths can serve at least this one purpose.

'But then, things are not the way they used to be when I was young. In the last few years everything's been changing as if we're waking up from hundreds of years of slumber. Shudras entered the temples first and then schools, colleges, and offices. They've become students, even teachers. The only ones who are yet standing like stagnant water are the Koosas and the Koragas. Except for a few here and there, most of them haven't changed at all. But we can't predict what might happen in another twenty to twenty-five years from now. Time stood still for a long, long time but is now racing ahead. My people are waking up. They've lost the age-old arrogance that had kept them to themselves. All they can do now is live in the world within their threshold and fret about losing the tuft on their heads. They can't do anything else. The people of my generation are the remnant of those whose mindset had

---

[1] gojju: gravy

been trained and nurtured to believe in their traditional values. Once *we* die, the change will come in much faster.

'Parthakka is fine in her own way but I don't like the things she tells the children about caste purity and pollution. If she sows such false notions in their impressionable minds, they might take on fearful forms later. Anyway her time is drawing to a close. Can't she realize that times are changing, especially after Bhaskara did what he did? ... But when *I* find it so difficult to accept the change, wouldn't it be wrong for me to expect *her* to accept them? If I try to talk to her about it she might even say, "Why, is it too much for you to have me in your home?"'

The last time Vasudevaraya visited Bhaskara he said as they sat down to dinner, 'I feel it's my duty to tell you, Bhaskara. Your mother's shattered by what you've done. She mopes every day.'

'Why, Mavaiyya, if she's upset only because I married a Korathi, I don't mind that at all,' replied Bhaskara, 'Now you tell me, which sub-sect of Brahmins do you think is superior to the rest?' Vasudevaraya wondered what he was getting at. Their conversation seemed to be taking a different turn; he did not know how to answer him.

'Look at it this way,' continued Bhaskara, 'If you as a Kota Brahmin get an offer of marriage for Saroja from a Shivalli Brahmin family, you may not say, "O, I won't give my daughter to those Tulu-speaking Brahmins." That's because Kotas and Shivallis do inter-marry these days. But there was a time when they didn't, only because they belonged to different sub-sects. Even the Shivallis felt the same way about marrying into Kota families. They said, "We don't want to have anything to do with those who say Hoikambru-Barkambru[2] *for go* and *come*. Is that any way to speak Kannada?" Look at the illusions we have about ourselves, Mavaiyya! We see one another as different because we speak Tulu or different dialects of Kannada! And I'm talking of only a few sub-sects of Brahmins who belong to the Dakshina Kannada and Udipi districts of Karnataka—Kota, Shivalli, Havyaka, Kandaavara, Koteshwara Maagane.... Each sect thinks it's superior to the rest. And all of us together feel the Maaleru are inferior to all of us. Why? If you trace the source, you'll find it's because they're supposed to be descended from the child of a

---

[2] Hoikambru-Barkambru: ridiculing a local dialect of Kannada

widow. Even if that is true, how can you respect people who consider them as a different sub-sect, *lower* than the rest? And as for the Pataali sect who keep the temple clean and get everything ready for worship, we've denied them the right to eat with us; we make them sit in a separate row, in the adda-pankthi. And we're the people who proclaim, Sahanaavavathu, Sahanou bhunakthu—May we all prosper together and grow in spirit!'

'But, Maharaya, who are *we* to question these things? Did *we* make the rules? It's a tradition we've followed. That's all, isn't it? If those whom we've demeaned sit and eat in the row we've set apart for them instead of protesting, is it *our* fault?'

'Mavaiyya, don't talk that way. I may get furious. Will those that call them inferior allow them to stand up and fight? It's the mind-set. For generations we've been saying to them, "You're inferior to us. You're inferior...." That notion is stuck in their heads and so they say, "Yes, you're superior to us" and treat us with deference. Not just that. *They've* also kept within *their* limits and have taught their children to respect the boundaries. *They* restrict *their* way of life to *their* framework. But we can continue to sow such ideas in them only until they wake up to the injustice of it all. I'm not saying only we Brahmins are guilty of being divisive. Peep into the depths of any caste. You'll find layers and layers of levels. Take the Koragas themselves. We think they're the lowest of the lowest. But the Kappadada Koragas[3] think of themselves as superior to the Soppina Koragas[4] only because they wear clothes, not leaves. If a Soppina Koraga goes to his house a Kappadada Koraga gives him water in a coconut shell. Not because they have only coconut shells for glasses but because these Koragas see the Soppina Koragas as the lower among the lowest of the lowest. What do you say to *that* now? If that isn't a farce, what is? Once we believe this to be the truth, we forget that Man made these distinctions in the first instance and we drag even God down to this level. People believe in God only to make a show of their devotion; to shower flowers on Him and press their palms together in obeisance. The earth will find no respite from the sins of people who worship Him for such display.'

---

[3] kappadada Koraga: Koraga who wears clothes

[4] soppina Koraga: Koraga who wears leaves

'Bhaskara, when you talk this way, I get the feeling you believe in God. I mean, in sin and righteousness and such things.'

Bhaskara laughed. 'It's not like that at all, Mavaiyya. These are sounds that roll off my tongue without its knowledge because Amma has used them over and over again. I say sounds because they're mere sounds as far as I'm concerned; sounds without any meaning. Sin could be wrong-doing, crime. We could be wrong in the way we conceive God. Isn't it enough to live an honest life without hurting another? Isn't it unnecessary to worry our heads about the existence of God? If God does exist, I feel sorry to see the way He's dragged about among men.'

Bhaskara's wife kept serving them silently. Her name was Thukri but he had changed it to Kumudhini. He had fought hard against his prejudice; he knew it was wrong to change her identity. But he had lost the battle.

'I've heard of yet another kind of Brahminism,' continued Bhaskara, 'Long ago, somewhere in the womb of history, the ancestors of these people thrashed an old lady to death and threw her body in a well. Since that day, these people are called Holeya Brahmins. What does that mean, Mavaiyya? That the Holeyas are murderers? That Brahmins don't murder? That despite being murderers, despite harbouring emotions that can make them kill, they've been given the concession to be Brahmins? Isn't this stupidity? Affection, love, lust, hate are basic to human nature. Some make it public, others keep it private. Those who were powerful could cover up their vices; those who couldn't, lost their caste and became a laughing-stock. This hasn't happened only among our people. Go among the hill-folk. It gets funnier. Orthodox Lingayats don't let Brahmins into their kitchen or puja-room. Did you know that? Now, who's higher, who's lower, you tell me?'

Vasudevaraya did not answer his question. Instead he said to Bhaskara's wife, 'Hudugi, you've cooked a great meal! You're now our own girl.'

'What's so great about learning to cook, Mavaiyya? Pretty soon we'll be able to teach a robot to cook a perfect Kota meal. And then will you bestow a caste on it calling it a Kota Brahmin robot?' Bhaskara laughed at his own joke. But the question did not sound like a joke to Vasudevaraya. He felt it had shaken the very roots of his being.

Bhaskara continued talking, unaware of the impact he was making on his guest, 'I'm not saying all this with any rancor against any caste, Mavaiyya. The very gods whom men have created were from different castes—Rama is a Kshatriya; Krishna was brought up in a cowherd's family. They became casteless only after they attained divinity. Doesn't it mean that the primal power, the aadhishakthi, is beyond caste? How did this world, supposedly created by a casteless God, get trapped in caste? I don't think things were so difficult in the beginning. Take the times of the Puranas, for instance. Valmiki was a hunter. Narada initiated him to spiritual life and he wrote the Ramayana. People eagerly accepted Ramayana written by a hunter. Isn't that true? I feel their social system was different from ours. People might've been classified according to their social responsibility and profession. Whoever started it and whyever they started it, look at the form it's taken now with all sorts of repercussions from its latest avatara.'

Dinner was almost over. Vasudevaraya felt he had had enough. Whichever way they turned, there seemed to be no way out of the maze. He knew he *had* changed quite a bit, no doubt, but he also knew there was no way he would change any more. He had listened to Bhaskara's *harikathe*[5] all this while but tomorrow, if Saroja were to say she wanted to marry someone from the halay-paika, would he be ready to give her to a Shudra? Vasudevaraya shuddered to see how deeply even *he* was rooted in the caste system.

Bhaskara, however, had not finished yet, 'Ultimately, do you know what all this boils down to, Mavaiyya? Impurity is unacceptable from anyone, anywhere, whether in speech or in action. If we call such inner cleanliness caste, how many will we find belonging to it, even if we search the whole world?'

'This is all very well, Maharaya. You've talked your head off as usual, but how long is it since you got married? Your mother was fretting to Gowri that you haven't had a child yet. What is this? In seeing to your responsibility towards others have you forgotten your responsibility to yourself?' Vasudevaraya teased him alluding to a bit of news in Sheena's letter. Bhaskara did not reply. He only laughed.

[5] harikathe: a narration of myths and legends to the accompaniment of music and song. Here, it refers sarcastically to the repetition of the same old story.

eleven

Genda

'Amma, Seethu says she'll take us to the genda. May we go? May we go and see people walk on glowing ember, Amma?' Shami, Jaya, and Putta were after Gowramma, pestering her to let them go with Seethu. Putta's feet refused to stand still, they danced up and down with excitement—thakka-thaiyya.[1] Would they leave her in peace if she refused to send them? No, they tailed her, holding on to the pallu of her sari, pleading with her. It wouldn't help even if she slapped them. To get out of a sensitive situation, she said, 'Ask Sarojakka. You can go if she says yes.'

'What's this?' Parthakka butted in. 'Going to the genda? Isn't there any other place you could go to? Only Shudras go there. You can't go to such places!'

'Of course! Of course!' Saroja was at her sarcastic best, 'Only Shudras can go to find out why the cows and buffaloes in Brahmin houses haven't calved. Why can't *we* go, Parthakka?'

'Henne, you talk too much. Can we find the right answers to all our questions? Why do you think there's One above? We have to live the way He's prescribed or else we may have to lose our eyes or hands or legs.'

[1] thakka-thaiyya: rhythm of dancing feet

'That's a lie! Amma, let them go today. They've been eager to see the genda for so long. If it's a sin for us to go there, let that burden be on me.'

Gowramma did not know what to say. 'Do what you children please. Don't get me into all this,' she said, washing her hands off the business.

Seethu called out to Parthakka from the yard, 'Why can't you send them, Parthamma? Forget about eating meat, we don't eat even fish today; we're that clean. Don't be scared. Send them.'

'*You* are the trouble-maker. Aren't you the one who set up the children? They were playing on their own, quietly. You always do what you shouldn't.'

'How can you say that, Amma? Didn't *you* get me to offer a rooster on your behalf to Kodi Amma last time because that Thunga didn't become pregnant despite her mating calls...?' As she recalled the fowl she had sacrificed on Parthakka's behalf, Seethu forgot about the cow that could not conceive. 'O, what a rooster that was! A nice, fat cockerel, Amma! My mouth waters even now. These days, we can't buy such a rooster for even twenty-five rupees. How we ate and ate and ate, my mother, my children and I.'

Putta, who stood there sucking his thumb, swallowed his spit.

Parthakka noticed that and said, 'Ei, all your talk about your fish and chicken has to be outside the gate. You cannot talk about them here,' and turning to Putta, 'Mani, where's Shiva?'

'I don't know. He was in the attic repairing the drawer of the table.'

'Go and call him.'

Putta ran so fast that anyone in his way would have been pulverized. He brought Shiva back with him. Shiva stood as if he knew nothing of what was going on.

'Mani, these children want to go to the genda. Seethu has got them all excited. Go with them. What will *they* know? They'll eat whatever she asks them to eat and drink whatever she gives them to drink. Stupid cockroaches!'

'Never! The other day when you asked me not to eat anything in the midbai's house, I didn't eat even a bit of bread. You know that, don't you, Parthakka?' reminded Shami.

'I've got some work to do,' said Shiva.

'You always have something or the other to do. Go with them, Shiva,' said Saroja. She didn't know he was already in league with the younger ones. Anyway, they set out.

'The genda at Kodi isn't like any other genda,' Seethu began, 'Only those who've been to it can know how powerful it is. However stubborn may be the spirit that possesses the cattle, it's enough to make a vow to the Kodiamma, she'll make it run away like one possessed. You can ask her for anything, even to bring back a husband who's deserted his wife and gone away to the hills. That Koggappa's daughter recovered only after offering prayers to Kodiamma. She was given up for dead, wasn't she? And she was his only child. He'd have hanged himself if he had lost her. Why go so far as Koggappa? What about my own daughter, Lachcha? Will one mouth do to talk about all the things people tried to prevent her wedding? As soon as I told Kodiamma about it, the wedding was over with the ease of picking flowers. And not just that! She has had a baby every year. She is pregnant for the fifth one now. And her husband loves her like his own life....'

The children lost interest. 'You started telling us about Kodiamma and you're unravelling the story of your daughter's family,' grumbled Shami.

'That's what I'm trying to tell you. Can anyone say enough about the Kodigenda? Anyway, you'll see for yourselves. Which month is it now? Isn't it bhaaraath?[2] It must be bhaaraath because the genda happens in Kodi during bhaaraath. Is this the only place where the genda takes place? Amma is propitiated in Kaipadi, Badaakodi, Asodi, Kallagara.... And how many Ammas do you want? There's Chikkamma, Maralu Chikku, Kodiamma....'

Listening to Seethu's yarns, the children felt no strain in walking up hill and down dale crossing pits and bridges. Evening was crawling towards night as they neared Kodi. 'The dhakke-bali[3] is towards the morning. That's when they sacrifice fowls to fulfil vows to Amma for

---

[2] margashira or bhaaraath: December, winter, the genda ritual

[3] dhakke-bali: a ritual of animal or bird sacrifice as thanksgiving for favours received

favours received. Didn't I sacrifice a chicken last year for Thunga, your cow? The genda takes place only at night.' Even as she was talking, Seethu saw that they were passing by Appu Poojari's coconut grove. 'Wait here,' she said and called out to Appu Poojari to bring down few tender coconuts for the thirsty children. As soon as he heard they were Vasudevaraya's children, Poojari said, as he climbed the tree with ease, 'Sit awhile, makkale. I'll get them down in a moment.' He brought down a bunch of tender coconuts fell—*dudum, dudum*.... He cut them open. The children drank the sweet cool water, ate the tender meat of the coconut, and felt refreshed. All except Putta, that is. He had poured more water on his shirt and the ground than into his mouth.

'Your shirt is wet and sticky. And it's a new shirt,' said Shami.

'Who are you to tell me that? Are you Amma? I know it's new. As soon as we reach home Seethu will wash it for me,' retorted Putta, leaning against Seethu.

'Haaa ... you touched Seethu! Wait till I tell Amma. Wait till I tell her,' Jaya jumped up and down where she stood, pointing and accusing all at once and vigorously.

'Channamma, don't you have anything better to do than fight? What if he touches me? Am I not human? Whether you touch me or you don't, Parthamma will, anyway, mix cow dung in water and pour the slurry over you to make you madi,' said Seethu, laughing as she walked on with Putta's hand in hers.

One of her friends called out, 'Who's that, Seethu? Your grandson?'

'No! Isn't he our Gowramma's son?' But by then Putta had lost face—how could that woman have thought he was Seethu's grandson? He withdrew his hand from Seethu's and moved away even if she tried to get near him. Seethu was amused by his embarrassment. Shami and Jaya teased him, a good excuse for a verbal fight.

Shiva had been walking at a distance. Seeing the children quarrel without giving Seethu an anna's worth of respect, he came back to stop the fight. By this time Putta was crying and his nose was running.

After they had walked further, Shami asked as if she had suddenly thought of something, 'Ei, Seethu, if I ask Kodiamma, will she help me pass my exams?'

'Oho, why won't she?' said Shiva, 'But don't promise a chicken. Just say you'll send four annas through Seethu next year. I'll recommend your case.'

'What's this, Shivayya? Is it something to joke about? We shouldn't make fun of Kodiamma, don't you know?'

'I know,' said Putta with fear in his voice, 'People who laugh at Amma will spit blood on the way and die.'

'How else do you think painter Basava died? He died on this very same street spitting blood while making fun of Kodiamma, didn't he?'

'Where? Where exactly? Did you see him spitting blood? Did you see with your own eyes, Seethu?' Putta asked, feeling the heat of fear in his ears.

'Of course, I saw him with these very eyes. He was walking ahead and I was right behind him. And people were milling all around us, all of us going to the genda. He died in front of all of us. Everything happened in a moment; he fell, his eyes rolled backwards, he died.'

'Stop it! Don't scare the children. Who knows what he was ailing from? He walked in the sun, didn't he? So he collapsed and died.'

'Shivanna, you stop it. I'm frightened,' whined Putta, with hardly any strength in his voice.

'Channayya, you don't have to be scared at all. I'm here with you,' assured Seethu.

Shami and Jaya made a pact, a vow to offer a coconut and some bananas jointly in thanksgiving to Kodiamma if she helped them pass their exams.

It was dark by the time they reached Kodi. The pit for the genda was spread over with burning coal. Kodiamma was being worshipped inside. At the end of the puja, the spirit of Kodiamma entered the paathri and he stepped out, swaying from side to side. There was a man on either side of him. The paathri held a singara[4] in each hand. He shook with frenzy as if he was boiling over. He pranced about here and there, swaying and swirling the fronds of areca flowers until he took a giant

---

[4] singara: frond of areca flowers

leap into the pit of live coal and walked across it. He landed with such force on the ember that bits of burning coal flew off the pit and landed on the onlookers as they deftly stepped aside. Silence mingled with fear enveloped the scene. The paathri sprinkled theertha on the genda and then his assistants began to call out the names of those who were fulfilling their vows to Kodiamma.

'They'll call out the names of those from the upper castes first,' whispered Seethu, 'and then the ones from the lower castes. The Koosas and the Koragas, of course, have no place here.' In that eerie ambience, it seemed better if she had not spoken at all. Somehow, her whispers made everything all the more scary.

'Look at the soles of the feet of those who're walking on the embers, makkale. The fiery coal hasn't burnt them at all. Those who vow to walk on fire have to follow strict rules the previous day. They shouldn't eat meat or fish. They shouldn't touch unclean people like women having periods, the Koosas and the Koragas, not even walk on the shadows of such people. They shouldn't even talk to them. If they break any of these rules, they'll surely get blisters.'

Putta gazed at the scene sucking his thumb. The same ritual happened over and over again, however much he stared at it; the paathri gave theertha and prasada to all those who had walked on the bed of fire. The children were beginning to feel drowsy. 'Come, let's go home. Enough of this,' they said.

On the way home, they were frightened of ghosts that walk in the dark, and of creepy-crawlies that might get under their feet. As Seethu put it, the children were so scared that their mouths were dry. They kept talking about what they had seen to feel the surprise afresh, over and over again. Shiva kept slamming his left fist into his right palm wondering, 'How could it be? How is it that the men didn't get blisters? How is this possible?' He walked ahead, trying to find an answer where there was none; it was a knot he could not unravel. If he had asked Seethu, she would have only said, 'Who do you think Amma is?'

They reached home at last. Putta was about to rush indoors as soon as he climbed the steps to the veranda.

'Stop right there, mani!' cried Parthakka, 'Don't come into the house. Go to the bathroom first. Who knows how many people you've touched!' All the children walked around the house to the bathroom at the back.

Vasudevaraya was angry. 'Why did you send the children to the genda? Didn't you have any thought that they might get frightened of the paathri?' he asked no one in particular. Only Saroja had the courage to calm him down. Gowramma told Seethu about it while Parthakka was engrossed in ritually cleanzing Putta. She mixed a ball of cow dung as big as a lemon in a big pot of water and poured the slurry over Putta till he could hardly breathe.

'Shami, Jaya, take off your clothes and pour water like this on each other,' she said, 'I've kept some balls of dung for you too. Mix it in the water. I'll ask Saroja to get you some clean clothes.' And she hobbled as fast as her arthritic knees would let her to get hold of Putta who had scampered off before she could dry his hair. Shiva was nowhere to be seen. When he did come in, she asked, 'Mani, have you cleansed yourself?'

'Oho, didn't you see me? Wasn't I the first one to come in?' he asked to side-track her.

Everyone laughed to hear of Putta becoming Seethu's grandson.

Seethu washed the children's clothes and hung them out to dry. 'When I go home, I'll pour a few pots of water over my head to get rid of my myligay,' she said.

'Why do *you* need to pour water over yourself? You're a Shudrathi anyway, aren't you? Oho, is it because Putta touched you?' Jaya shot an arrow for amusement.

But Gowramma was not amused. 'What kind of talk is that, henne? Why should she bathe if Putta touched her? When girls talk, their words should carry weight.'

'Why should I cleanse myself if Puttayya touches me, Channamma? Am I not purified by his very touch,' Seethu began to explain, 'But listen to what happened to me on our way back. When we crossed the grove, didn't you see a group of Koragas on their way to Koppa, their settlement? The sari of one of those wretches touched me however much I moved away from her. I'll have no peace until I wash my hair now.'

'But why, Seethu? When I touched you, didn't you say with the same mouth, "What if he touches me? Am I not a person like you?" Aren't the Koragas too people like you?' Putta sounded vehement.

'You won't understand all this, Ayya. They're people who eat leftovers, who clean latrines. Can the people of that caste ever be equal to us?' said Seethu as she walked away briskly.

The children could talk only about the genda as they lay in bed after dinner.

'Putta is dark as dark can be. That's why people think he's Seethu's son.' This was from Jaya.

'As if you're very fair-skinned!' Putta was spoiling for a fight. But they could not fight for long. They knew their father was in the very next room. He would scold them if he heard them.

Putta was anyway drifting into deep sleep. 'Shiva didn't spit blood and die after all, did he?' he asked sleepily.

In the terrifying quiet of the night, his soft voice sent a shiver through the rest. Shami slapped Putta, asking him to shut up. Putta sat up, shocked, 'What did *I* say?' He lay down again after they told him. But he had been startled awake and could not sleep.

'Ei, Shivanna, why can't we touch those people?' asked Jaya.

'Nothing will happen if we touch them. That's just nonsense,' replied Shiva, 'I don't know how many times Duggu's children and I have touched one another whenever we rehearsed our plays. What's happened? Nothing! When they act smart even I act smart with them. That's about all.'

But Shami did not like the way Shiva talked.

'They stink of fish. Don't you know? They don't bathe even once in three days.'

'Then, can we touch them if they come home after a bath?' Jaya wanted to know.

'But they *don't* bathe.' There was finality in Shami's answer.

'Also, they were shed from God's feet.' Putta added his bit from Parthakka's stories to shed some light on the problem.

'From His *feet*? How's that?' Jaya wanted to know more.

'Ei, don't you know even that much? Have you forgotten what Amma said about how we were born? Didn't we rise from her feet to her stomach? All of us were in the tips of her toes. Then her toes were chubby. Then, one by one we rose to her belly, split it open and came out.'

'How many are there in the tips of her toes, then?'

'She said there aren't any more after Putta came out.'

'*Aisaa!*' Putta smacked his lips. He was going to be the youngest forever.

'Most probably, God's toes might've bloated too. Perhaps the Shudras wanted to slit open the toes and come out. Maybe when they slit it open, all of them fell out together.'

'Ayyabba! Can you imagine how fat God's feet must've been in the beginning of beginning?' Putta asked a question he could not comprehend, throwing the rest into confusion.

'Ai, don't say, devara kaalu for God's feet. Say devara paada. Paada sounds more respectful,' scolded Shami.

'Maybe Seethu's caste came from God's big toe and the Koosas and Koragas from God's small toe. Or else, why would Seethu say she can't touch them?'

They mulled it over but could not find a solution. In fact, the more they pondered over it, the more complicated it became. They did not even know when they drifted off to sleep.

twelve

Marriageable Girls

As soon as she woke up, Shami sat on the stairs to the attic and looked out. She could see the front yard, levelled with rusty red pipe clay and the smoothed out patch right in front of the house, blackened with cow dung water mixed with chimney soot. Dhoopa flowers had fallen everywhere; white stars spread like a blanket on the black floor. Their heady scent reached her. If only she could lie on them! She looked this way and that. No one was around. She sneaked outside and lay on the bed of flowers facing the sky. She glanced sideways. Just a little away from the dhoopa, there stood the devadharu, laden with flowers, rose-coloured and ornamental, like a decorated temple chariot with jet-black pods hanging down from it. Cattle loved the pods that grew out of these flowers. Whenever they could, Jaya and Shami carried home as many pods as they could find on their way back from school. They went straight to the shed to feed the cows even before going inside for coffee. Wherever else they may be chewing grass, the cows had to hear just one pod being thrown in for them to go towards Jaya and Shami to be fed. Sometimes the girls were lucky if they were able to get at least one twig of pods. Looking for pods took them almost half an hour to get home. There was no respite from their mother's scoldings for coming late.

Shami lay flat on her back soaking in the silence. And then she remembered, 'Ayyo, they say we shouldn't lie facing the sky. If a bird flies over us, we'll be crippled in one leg, they say.' She turned to a side. She rolled over. The flowers tickled her. Their scent stung her nostrils. 'If only I'd been born a dhoopa flower!'

Rukku came by with a broom. 'What is this, Shamamma? Don't you have anything else to do but roll on flowers even before brushing your teeth?' She watched her, amused. 'Okay, are you satisfied now? Get up, get up. If your mother sees you like this, that'll be the end of you.'

'O, Rukku, please don't sweep them away. They're so beautiful!'

'But what if Amma scolds me?'

'If Amma scolds you tell her I asked you not to. Shami mumbled as if she were dreaming.

'Then, shall I go and tell her right away?' As soon as Shami saw Rukku walking away, she got up as if from a dream and hastily dusted her clothes.

'What's nice about them, Shamamma? Let them see the sun. They'll shrivel up and stink. Then even I can't sweep them up.'

The bed of white starry flowers disappeared in a moment. Shami stared at nothing. Once the nuts appear, Shiva would have only two things to do, pick them up and crack them open. The pockets of his khaki uniform would be stuffed with them. Putta, Jaya, and Shami too gathered as many as they could but their nuts were never as good as Shiva's. Shiva would stick a nut in the door and press the door on it hard until it cracked it open. He would remove the kernel and hand it to the young ones. Ganapathi-like kernels! Rose-coloured! Putta always got the best Ganapathi. How easy it was to snatch it from him! ... But their father had told them not to grab something that belongs to someone else. That thought always sat in a corner of their minds. Shiva pocketed the good nuts in the twinkle of an eye and cracked open only the bad ones for his sisters. If one of them said, 'This one's no good, it's blanched. Give me the pink one in your hand,' he would say, 'Yes, yes, I'll give it to you, look at the sky,' pointing his forefinger upwards. And in all these transactions, who'll remember school?

'What is this, Shami? What's happened to you today? Don't you have to go to school? You haven't had your bath yet.' Only when the voice floated out from inside did Shami come out of her reverie. In a tearing hurry, she had her bath, dressed for school, had her milk and ganji for breakfast, held her books to her chest; ready to set off. 'Amma, I'm going,' she shouted.

Saroja was sweeping the veranda. 'Ei, come here,' she said, 'Turn around.'

'What's it, Sarojakka? It's getting late for school,' said Shami, turning her back to Saroja.

'Amma ...,' called Saroja, her voice soft yet urgent.

'What is it?'

'Come here, Amma. Everything else can wait. Come soon.'

Gowramma hurried out anxiously and stopped short, staring at Shami's skirt, 'O, another thorn!' was all she said.

'Amma, you still haven't stopped saying such things,' grumbled Saroja.

'Sarojakka, what is it now? I'll be late for school. Why did you call me?' Shami sounded peevish.

'I called to tell you, you needn't go to school today,' said Saroja, smiling.

'O, that can't be. The exams are coming. They'll give us piles of notes.'

'Come here,' said Saroja gently and whispered in her ear. Shami flopped to the floor and burst into tears as if a great calamity had struck her down. And what a weeping that was! With sighs and shudders, the tears gushed out.

'Maharayithi, we don't need your histrionics on *this* stage. Come inside. What's happened that you should cry so much? This happens to every girl, doesn't it?' That was Gowramma's way of comforting her daughter. Turning to Saroja, she said, 'Take her to the small room, Saroja. Let her sit there. Give her a piece of cloth and teach her what to do with it.' Shami left her books on the veranda and went into the small room, still crying.

'How worried I used to be every time she returned from school. Lately the girl was blossoming so well. That Phaniyammajji, who brings the avadekodu beans actually asked the other day if she had come of age. That old woman has to know everything that happens all over town. Anyway, I'm glad this happened before she left for school. There's only Jaya left now. Don't know when that will happen.'

'Amma, I remember what you did to Rathnakka and me. We ate in that dark room; we washed our hands in there. We couldn't have a bath for three days! Couldn't even comb our hair! Shee ... shee.... I wasn't as docile as Akka. I turned your madi upside down. Shami will be worse. She won't listen to you even as much as I did.'

'Henne, what do you know about these things? We had to bathe even if the shadow of a girl having her periods fell on us. Of course, we're not *that* fussy about madi now. But shouldn't we do at least as much as we can?'

'No need, Amma. Shami can stay there because she needs the rest. I don't think it's fair for us to bother her with madi and mylige. There's no need to dip her palms in a mixture of turmeric powder and quicklime and make those reddish imprints of them on the bathroom wall like you did for me. No need for the arathi too. Is this something unusual that's happened to her? Isn't it what happens to every girl the wide world over? You're the one who says, there's no need for anyone to know and you're also the one who does all these rituals and lets everyone know. Let her be, Amma. She's already upset.

'But that's not the right thing to do, Saroja. When *I* had my periods for the first time, a large number of guests from my husband's family came home. They brought milk and ghee ... made imprints of my palms on the wall. This is the way these things are done.'

'Make some special snacks. Who asked you not to? But don't invite people for an arathi. There's no need for that kind of fuss.'

'What's this I hear? Shami's come of age, has she?' asked Parthakka even as she stepped into the house. She had returned from her morning ritual of going round the peepul tree. 'Rukku told me. I told her not to beat the drum all over town.'

'That's because of Saroja. Shouldn't she have taken Shami straightaway into the small room as soon as she had seen what had happened? No, she had to stand right here and investigate. If Rukku knows, it's like letting loose the fragrance of kasturi in the wind.'

'A fine person you are, Amma! If I hadn't noticed it, she'd have gone to school. When she said, "Amma, I'm off to school," didn't you say, "Go"?'

'But I was cooking, wasn't I? I didn't even turn to see her go. Do I have eyes on my back?'

Both of them got worked up. There was no sense in what they were saying; meaningless words spoken in the heat of the moment to keep the fight going until it could wear itself out. They argued for quite a while.

Shami had been taught what she had to do. She had not stopped crying. Gowramma was upset, 'Until now the child had one kind of life. Now what? It's going to be, "don't go there, don't go here, don't come home after dark, stay at home, get married, beget babies, look after daughters who beget babies...." By the time you're through with all this you'd be spent and old enough to sit and be served. Isn't this what being a woman is all about?'

But Saroja would not agree. 'That's because *we've* made it this way.'

'Henne, don't fly too high,' cautioned Parthakka, 'A woman is a woman, after all. Say a man holds you down when you're walking down the street. What'll you do? People may beat him, they might even kill him. How will it help? *You* would've lost your honour for ever, wouldn't you? You can never get it back whatever you do.'

'It's not that easy to hold anyone down, Parthakka. Moreover, honour is how we understand it. If he tries to grab my honour, it's *he* who'll lose his honour not me. I'll sue him for abusing me. Let him try.'

'Yes, yes, you do deserve a prize for bragging, don't you?'

Shami sat staring at Saroja.

'And Shami, you have to stop being playful, henne,' Parthakka turned on Shami, 'When you go about hold your skirt close to you ... for three days. You know what girls having periods are? They're Koosas the first day, Chandalas the second day, and on the third day, Bhrahmarakshasis.'

Shami's wails filled the air.

'There's no need to weep so much. If you abide by the rituals, God will see you through,' Parthakka tried to comfort her. Saroja started to say something but stopped. She stared at Parthakka, got up, and left the room.

When Jaya came home for lunch she said, 'Shami's friends asked why she hadn't come to school.'

'Tell them she has fever.'

'Does she have fever?' Putta got up immediately to go and see his sister.

'Don't touch her. Her fever will come to you. Eat quickly and go to school,' Gowramma dragged him back and sat him down to eat.

After he returned that evening, Putta went about asking questions, getting answers and putting them together to make some sense. Gowramma and Parthakka were busy in the kitchen making special snacks for the occasion. He sat on his haunches on the threshold of Shami's room, peered into the darkness to spot her, and whispered, 'Ei, Shamakka, they say you've started your periods. Have you?' Shami started sobbing. Putta stared at her for a while. 'What does it mean? ... Jayakka also wants to know.'

'Shee, shee, get away,' said Shami, still weeping. Putta felt like wiping her eyes. But he couldn't touch her, could he? 'I can't touch you. Why, Akka?' Shami could not answer him. Her sobs got worse. 'Don't cry. Amma's made different kinds of sweets. I'll go and get you an unde,' said Putta as he got up to go.

As he slept next to Parthakka that night, he made her laugh telling her about this, that and the other and then asked her softly, 'Parthakka, tell me the truth. What does it mean to have periods? Why shouldn't we touch those who've had periods?' Equally softly, Parthakka replied, 'Don't tell anyone, okay? If a white crow touches a person, she has her periods. People who touch them will turn into black crows and fly away.'

'Then, the crows that come to our house? Is that the way they happened?'

'Then? How else could we have black crows? Don't you go and touch her, okay.'

'Hm,' mumbled Putta, gathering his coverlet closer in fear.

Jaya who lay listening on the other side of Parthakka asked, 'But why does the white crow touch only girls? Boys don't have periods, do they?'

'Is that any question for a *girl* to ask? What do you think men are? How can crows ever touch *them*? Sleep quietly.'

Shami wore a dhavani now. She did not spend the whole day in the backyard or on trees as she used to. She had become subdued. She spent time inside the house working out problems in geometry, memorizing lessons, or doing some simple embroidery. But she had become short-tempered and moody. If anyone tried to say something like, 'That's not the way to behave, maga,' she walked away in a huff. If ever Putta asked her something, she replied to him once in a new moon or maybe once in a full moon. On other days, she would say, 'Why do you bother me?' so sharply that his question would fly away in fright. If he persisted, she would pinch him hard on his arm when no one was looking. If he screamed in pain that Shami had pinched him, she would deny it belligerently, almost daring the arbitrator to protest. It looked as if she was in some turmoil. Everyone seemed like a stranger. All except Saroja. Only Sarojakka seemed to be able to reach out to her. Even Jaya who was a mere two years younger to her seemed so much younger mentally. Shami felt she was an in-between, neither a child nor an adult. Perhaps that was the reason for her confusion; perhaps it made her what she had become; stubborn, always spoiling for a fight. Though the others were relieved she had given up her childlike ways, Saroja felt Shami was holding her breath. And so, she made time to be with her; to chat with her. If anyone tried to advise or scold or argue with Shami when she flew into a temper, Saroja steered her away deftly and distracted her with other things. Then she said, very casually, 'What a temper you have, Shami! How upset you were over such a small thing! But your anger's not even a third of mine when I was your age.' Saroja knew that last bit was a lie.

'Really? I don't know why I get so furious, Sarojakka,' said Shami, opening up to her elder sister. With every word she spoke, her anger thawed, flowing out of her like water. By then, the sisters had forged a new bond, one of friendship.

Shami had come of age. Now there were two girls to be married. They would have to look for a bridegroom for Saroja. But what did that mean? Will he be lying somewhere on the wayside to be found? When the propitious time comes, the wedding would happen without any strain. However much Gowramma tried to find solace in that thought, every day she felt a shudder go through her whenever she saw Saroja going about her work, quiet, and withdrawn.

There was no point in talking about it with her husband; Vasudevaraya did not share her anxiety. He was not the kind to go knocking at other people's doors telling them he had a daughter to be married. If anyone did suggest a proposal he said he would consider it. If men who had daughters were so arrogant, is it possible for them to get their girls married? Gowramma felt helpless. She asked visitors if there were any suitable boys in their village. That upset Saroja, 'Amma, you won't be at peace until you get me married and see me through my first baby, will you? Why do you tell everyone who visits that I have to be married? Is it respectable?'

Saroja had spent a year at home after graduation. She should have been allowed to work. That would have been better. A girl's age does not show when she is doing something. Perhaps even the mother would not have been so preoccupied with getting her married. Some people were quite blatant. They did not hesitate to ask, 'Have you found a boy for Saroja?' But Gowramma took it in her stride, saying to Saroja, 'Why won't people ask if there's a girl or a boy in the house to be married? Why should you get so worked up?' In fact, there were times when she got angry with Saroja for being touchy, 'People who ask may ask until you get married and have a baby, perhaps. Later, they may ask where you're living and how many children you have. That's about all. What else will they ask? What else is there for them to ask? Everyone's life is just about the same, anyway.'

Gowramma found that girls were getting sensitive these days. If she said something, they took offence; if she did not, they were hurt. At times it seemed wrong even to open her mouth. And Saroja was just a bit too much. Gowramma could be relieved only after she cast her burden on someone else's head and washed her hands off her. But where could she find the right man? Where was Saroja's husband born? Saroja was on pins, eager to go to work. Gowramma had asked Rathna to ask her husband to find her a job. That way, there would be some truce in the house for some time. But she felt a chill when he said, 'Why does she need to work instead of getting married? If she gets a job and runs away with someone what'll you do? Once you lose your respectability, can you get it back even if you pay for it? You have other children to be married. Moreover, that daughter of yours talks too much. She's also stubborn. Nothing she does should surprise us. Girls shouldn't be so headstrong. It would be good for you to keep her under control right now.' He hardly ever spoke but when he did, not a single word was superfluous. As for that matter, what was wrong in what he said? Of course, it sounded harsh but it carried weight. It made sense to Gowramma. Be it bad times or good, they commanded respect; they had a good name. What could they live with if they lost that?

'Did my Ajjayya let me step out of the house before I got married?' thought Gowramma, fondly remembering her grandfather. 'And my Appayya and Annayya? Were *they* any different? According to them, girls were not allowed to go anywhere. Why, we couldn't even laugh loudly. They brought us up saying a girl's laughter shouldn't be heard by the roof tiles. If ever we laughed aloud while chatting, they'd growl, "What sort of whorish laughter is that? Planning to go to *Bombai*?"[1] And after hearing such words, we couldn't eat, couldn't drink. We'd be so upset with our misbehaviour, we'd shrink within ourselves. Yes, that's how it was then. The beam and rafters never heard our voices. We never crossed the threshold until we stepped out to go to our husbands' houses. Those were the days when we were unaware of anything but the wood-fire oven, the buttermilk-churner, the grinding-stone, and the way to make cattle-feed.

'And now? None of those things are important. Girls can hardly wait to fly out of the kitchen. They're not happy to stay indoors. Appayya used to say, "People must see your clenched fist and wonder what you have inside it. What's the fun in showing them an open hand? That's how the mystery of God's creation works. As long as women are like tightly closed fists, all will be well with caste, dharma, country ... everything will survive." There were elders to teach us such things, Ajji, Ajjayya, Amma, Appayya, Mavayya.... Why, such people are around even now. Isn't Parthakka here? Am I not here? And the children's father? But there's no one to listen to us. For everything we say, they have questions. Pointless questions—"Why? What will happen?" Is this what creation is all about; answering questions? Did *we* ever ask questions? Did any even sprout from us? Once spoken, the words of the elders were final. Will they ever say anything to harm us? Isn't it only proper for us to do as they say? There was no question of an alternative; a "What else can we do instead?" Even if a question did crop up here and there, who had the courage to

---

[1] Mumbai, used here as a city with its temptations

bring them out to the open? Is such courage worthwhile? Definitely not! The one who stands before her Appayya or Abbe and argues will go straight to hell. Which parent would like his child to go astray?

'What a good alliance we had for Saroja last year! The boy had so much! Enough to eat for two generations! And this girl refused him. Couldn't she think, "My Appayya's growing old, he has other obligations to fulfill; I have younger sisters to be married ...?" And she knows people are hesitant to strike a relationship with us because of Parthakka. What's the use of school, education, and learning to read and write if it doesn't teach such responsibilities? The problem is with him; *he's* not adamant enough. If I had said something like that to *my* father, he would've said, "Why? You'll *have to* marry him." That's it. He would've held me by the hair and dragged me to the mantapa. But *he*? He asked his daughter, "Would you like to marry him?" and she said, "No," and he actually listened to her! If we keep asking our daughters for their opinion, how can we get them married? Will girls ever say, "Yes?"? Why else do they say girls should be kept in their place?

'The other day she overheard me telling Parthakka what Rathna's husband had said about her. How furious she was! She flared up at him even though he was her bhava. She talked about how badly he had treated Rathna when she spent that week with them. She said she'd never accept the job even if he did find her one. How could she say such things? Whatever he may do to Rathna, how does it concern her? Rathna is his wife, his property. He hasn't strangled her, has he? Why did she have to interfere? Rathna was also upset. Wouldn't she have told her husband about it? He would've become bitter against Saroja. Not just that. She didn't even stay the fortnight she was supposed to; she came away earlier. What an insult! She's a bit stupid, this girl; she's not aware of the consequences of her actions.

'And such a girl wants to go out and work. She's been jumping up and down that she wants to. If I say she can't, she's sullen the whole day. I know she's frustrated sitting at home doing nothing and not getting any offers of marriage either but is her Ajja waiting to give her a job just because she's hopping on one toe? If there's an auspicious date in the offing, we must get her married off....'

Gowramma's worries seemed endless.

thirteen

The Headlines

Vasudevaraya's head reeled as he read the morning paper. This was what he had always feared: Bhaskara's arrest. There was no point in asking why. There were gangs of power-mongers behind this. But to think it had actually happened! Vasudevaraya called Shiva immediately and warned him, 'Mani, let's not tell anyone about this. Hide the paper. They'll get to know, anyway. Let that be. But there's no need for any commotion so early in the morning.'

Shiva read about Bhaskara's arrest. His hair stood on end. He had to tell someone. But whom? Hadn't Appayya told him not to tell anyone at home? Could he not keep a secret at least for the moment? Suddenly, he felt he was asked to shoulder adult responsibilities. And so the news that spread like wildfire all over town was arrested in the inner room. It could not enter the kitchen.

But Sheena arrived by lunchtime. 'Sheenanna's here! Sheenanna! Sheenanna!'

'What is it, mani? So unexpectedly? How's Bhaskara?' Vasudevaraya asked his questions amid the children's shouts of excitement.

'What can I say, Appayya?'

'Why does he get involved in such things? Does he need them? Trying to do good ... to people who won't even remember it,' Vasudevaraya said with some disgust mingled with some pride.

'Ei, mani, Sheena! What's this? Why are you standing there and talking? Come inside. How is it you've come so suddenly?' Gowramma let loose her stream of questions.

Sheena hung his bag on a nail and came in and said, 'What are you saying, Amma? Don't you know Bhaskaranna's in prison? Didn't Appayya tell you?'

'*What*! No, he didn't tell us at all.'

Now Shiva found it impossible to pretend to be a moron who knew nothing of what was happening around him. His belly was already bloated like a huge pot with the secret he was forced to keep. Moreover, he wanted to show off that he was old enough to know everything.

'I knew all about it. Appayya had told me not to tell anyone. You'd start wailing, he said.'

Putta needed only four strides to reach Parthakka who sat in the backyard breaking off the stalks from dried red chilies, 'Parthakka, Parthakka, Bhaskaranna's gone to prison. Sheenanna's come ...,' Putta rolled his eyes and gesticulated wildly to express the enormity of the news he was bringing her.

'Have you lost your head, mani?' said Parthakka weakly as she dashed the knife and board aside, pulled up the end of her sari that was slipping off her head, tucked it behind her ears, and stepped hastily into the house. Sheena was going outside to wash his feet. Everyone followed him. Everyone except Vasudevaraya.

'What, Sheena? Is it true? What Putta says,' Parthakka's voice was trembling.

'Yes, Parthakka, it's true. But there's no need for you to get so worked up. Wait a moment. Let me just wash my feet.' Sheena washed his hands and feet, had his coffee, and came and sat beside her.

'Why are you so terrified? Your son hasn't killed anyone. He hasn't robbed anyone. All he did was create some slight disturbances while fighting for the Koosas and the Koragas. That led to this kind of trouble. There was some commotion in town for some other reason. Those who were against Bhaskaranna lodged a false complaint saying he was the cause. That's why he's in prison.'

'Mani ... mani ...' Parthakka could not find words to clothe her anguish.

'Don't be sad, Parthakka. Your son's name is on the front page of today's paper. Do you know what that means? Make some *payasa*. It's a big thing to have his name in the papers. Shouldn't we celebrate with a sweet dish?' said Shiva.

'Shiva, there's a time and occasion for jokes and fun. *Shut up!*' Gowramma was upset.

'Why, Amma? Did you think Shiva was joking?' asked Sheena, 'We have to be proud of Bhaskaranna for going to prison for *this* reason.'

'Okay, let's feel proud. Then, why aren't *you* with him? Why are you out? You too could've joined him in his disturbances, couldn't you? What else will boys like you do if you don't have anyone to check you? Do you know what it means to go to jail? It's like slipping and falling in front of people who're laughing at you. As it is we had some people talking about us. Now we've become the talk of every street.' Gowramma was getting angrier by the moment.

'... Mani, Sheena, I don't think it's entered your head that Saroja isn't yet married because you have *me* in your house,' put in Parthakka, 'And now, there's this as well. What does Bhaskara have in mind? Is it that his mother shouldn't live peacefully even here? I haven't stepped into his house. How can he bring disgrace to your father who's given shelter to this old woman who's now without *kula*, without *gothra*? Is he my son?'

Saroja had been standing silently, taking in what was going on. Now she spoke, 'Look here, Parthakka. If my wedding hasn't happened because of Bhaskaranna, let it just be. If any man doesn't want to marry me just because Bhaskaranna has married a Korathi and has been working to support the Koosas and the Koragas, I too am not willing to marry such an adharmic person. For that matter, if Bhaskaranna were to bring an educated good-natured Koosa and ask if I'd marry him, I'd say, yes.'

'*Huun*, you'll say, "Yes," will you? What else will you say? Have you spared any thought for your younger sisters who are to be married after you?' Gowramma's voice raged with a fire she had never known before. 'We've been too lenient with you. That's our fault. We should've reined you in that very day Rathna's husband spoke about you that way. Are you a triloka sundari to say, "I won't marry *this* man, I won't marry *that* man?" We're not yet dead; we, who've begotten you. It's *your* dharma to get married to whoever *we* choose for you. Are you going to stay young forever? Before we look this way and that, you'll be thirty and you'll have sunken cheeks. And then, who'll marry you? Only a Koosa!'

'Chi! Chi!' Her mother's fury choked Saroja. She had never been scolded that way. She left the place wiping her nose.

Hearing Gowramma's unusual ranting, Vasudevaraya too came inside. 'What is this, Sheena? You never told me the details. And now you're sitting here like an idiot listening to their pointless raving.'

'What can I do, Appayya?'

'What can I do, Appayya?' Vasudevaraya imitated his son, 'As if you're still a child! Come, come in! Tell me all that's happened there. Is it any kind of news to be spoken about in the open?'

Sheena clasped his hands behind him and followed his father.

Shutting the window, Vasudevaraya drew up a chair and sat down.

'Out you go, all of you!' he barked.

The children did not want to and looked at each other.

'Can't you hear me if I tell you once?' Putta, Jaya, Shami slipped out quietly, one by one.

Putta came back, 'Appayya, Shivanna ...,' he said, pointing to his elder brother.

'Let him be!' said his Appayya. Putta's thumb went into his mouth.

Shiva wagged his forefinger at Putta as if to say, 'Serves you right.'

Sheena began ... 'It was about six in the evening by the time I got the news of Bhaskaranna's arrest. I went to his house immediately. Athigay was sitting there like a rock. She didn't even talk to me when she saw me. "Don't fret, Athigay," I said to her, "I'll find out what it's all about. Take heart." It took her some time to talk to me. "Your Bhaskaranna told me not to worry and to make arrangements with the hospital." Do you know, Appayya? Her baby's due this month.'

'What! Mani, is she pregnant! Did he have to worry about the world outside with a pregnant wife in the house? And she due to deliver any day!' Gowramma was very upset.

'Pregnant? What kind of a womb is it to bear the child! A casteless womb! A womb that deserves to be stoned!' Parthakka cursed in a voice that had lost its power.

'Parthakka! How can you say that?' growled Vasudevaraya as he turned towards her wondering if it was really Parthakka saying such things.

'How can you understand my grief, Maharaya? Having been born into such a fine family ...' she could not speak further.

'Why are you upset, Parthakka? If you get a grandson you could celebrate his upanayana for four days. Why do you say he shouldn't be born at all?' asked Shiva.

Gowramma did not like the liberties Shiva was taking with Parthakka. 'Who gave this boy permission to talk so much? Mani, you may stay here if you can keep your mouth shut or else I'll throw you out,' she said.

'Athigay did cry a bit when she told me that,' continued Sheena, 'But she's more composed now. She'll have the baby in the hospital where she's been going for her check-up. The same doctor will see to the birthing. I know everyone there. But I know what Athigay needs now though she doesn't seem to want anything. I can't bear to see her alone in her sadness. That's the reason I'm here. If you'll let me, I thought I could take at least Saroja to her.'

Vasudevaraya was thoughtful.

'What did you say?' Gowramma pounced on Sheena, her voice cracking with anger, 'You're taking Saroja, are you? Who do you think is going to send *her*? Not bad! You're trained quite well in his company, aren't you?' And then she said firmly, 'Mani, Saroja won't come with you. No one will go from this house to Bhaskara's for his sake. No one should go. Why? Did he think before he made her pregnant? Did he think he could lay the responsibility on someone else's head? If we're nothing to him, his wife and children too are nothing to us.'

'I thought I heard someone say "Saroja" and so here I am,' said Saroja as she walked in, addressing no one but everyone.

'It's nothing. No one asked you here. Leave the room,' said Gowramma.

'What happened to Amma today? What have I done that she should scold me so much? If you talk to me this way, Amma, I won't move from here.'

Sheena spoke to her directly, 'Saroja, Athigay's baby's due any day now. She's alone in the house. I thought I could take you ...'

'But why? Why should *I* go there? You could've brought *her* here, couldn't you?'

'What! What did you say, you cur? How *ever* did your tongue utter such words? Get out of here! Get out, I said! *Clear out!*' Gowramma's voice was heavy with fury, anguish. and contempt.

Then Parthakka who was ripening by the moment in her grief, said gently, 'Saroja, maga, youth comes to everyone. When it does, you don't care for the place of your birth or for your country. That's because your mind is not steady. That's how it is with you now. You don't know what you're saying. That girl doesn't deserve to climb the steps to this house, not in a thousand births. Remember that. In your haste to be known as a good girl, don't send the ancestors of your Appayya's family to hell.'

'We want Bhaskaranna. How can we say we don't want his wife?' asked Shiva sadly, unable to keep quiet.

'Who said we want Bhaskara? Do I want him now that he has set my belly on fire? Let him be damned somewhere!'

'Parthakka, I haven't thought of Bhaskara only as your son until now,' Vasudevaraya felt he had to explain his stand. 'I have a deeper connection with him. I respect him as the person who has the courage to do what I long to do but don't have the nerve to. That bonding is greater than this relationship where he's your son and she's your daughter-in-law. But you won't understand all that.'

'Vastheva, very soon you'll be sixty. You'll be celebrating your sashtipurthi. Are you still dancing to their tune? Shouldn't you be showing them the right path?'

'Let's not spend too much talk on this. Saroja is right. I'll go with Sheena and bring her here,' replied Vasudevaraya.

'*Haan*? What do you mean?' cried Gowramma, her voice tightening with tears. 'Are you trying to get us out of here? The Koragas live in Koppa. If they come to live in these storied houses, we may have to move to Koppa. No one in this town will touch us. In the heat of the moment, you may not realize what you're doing. You may have to repent later. Listen to me just this once.'

'Didn't I say there's no need to say anything more about this? When I say I'll bring her, I'll do just that. I'll bring her here.'

'If you do, the maid may stop working for us. Let's see who'll attend to the new mother? Who's going to do all the work in the house?'

'Appayya, I'll look after Bhaskaranna's wife. You fetch her,' said Saroja calmly.

Parthakka was shocked.

'Here, Vastheva! Don't do me this favour. You still have children to be married. Don't throw a boulder on their heads. Do you think this is child's play?' Parthakka's voice was rising to an anguished wail. 'Why was this boy born to me? Is it to hurt me so much? Vastheva, if you bring her here, I'll walk out of this home, go away somewhere far away and drown myself in some pond or well. Did you think I have enough life in me to live here enduring all this?'

'Appayya, even if you ask her to come here, Athigay may not want to,' said Sheena softly, too scared to open his mouth.

'When I ask you to be quiet, just stay quiet. Shiva, get my bag ready, mani. Sheena, we'll travel by the Apoorva Express that leaves here at two o'clock. All those who wish to go to Koppa may go before we return.' Gowramma got up and walked away, weeping noisily, pressing the pallu of her sari to her mouth.

The house held the silence of death during lunch. Gowramma did not come out to serve the meal. Neither she nor Parthakka ate anything.

'When will you return, Appayya?' asked Saroja.

'Whenever we do,' said Vasudevaraya as he set out.

fourteen

Thukri aka Kumudhini

By the time Vasudevaraya and Sheena reached Bhaskara's house it was nearly nine that night. Not wanting to bother Bhaskara's wife, they ate in a restaurant after getting off the train.

'Athigay!'

'Who? O, is it Shreenivasa? Coming!' said Bhaskara's wife coming slowly to the door.

Her name was Thukri but Bhaskara had renamed her Kumudhini at their wedding.

'Appayya's come!' said Sheena as he stepped inside. Vasudevaraya was right behind him.

'Are you well, magu?'

'Oho!' answered Kumudhini, pleasantly surprised. He had never called her magu before. 'Come in! Sit down! What's this? So unexpected.'

No one spoke for an awkward moment. Kumudhini stood wondering why Vasudevaraya had taken all the trouble to visit her.

'Ayyo, look at me! I haven't even given you anything to drink!' she exclaimed.

'Don't worry! We've just had our dinner. Come, sit down. There's so much that we need to talk about,' said Vasudevaraya.

As if something had just struck her, Kumudhini said, 'Ha, Shreenivasa, where have you been since the morning?'

'If you're trying to guess where I've been, I think you've got it right, Athigay. I'm the reason Appayya's here. I went home and told him exactly how things here are and he, on his own, decided to come with me.'

'What do you mean ... exactly how things here are?'

'Arre, how things here are means exactly how things here are. You know what I mean. But there's no need to talk about all that now. Ask why Appayya has come.' Sheena spoke with some pride, as if he had achieved something great.

Kumudhini looked at Vasudevaraya.

'Magu, I'll see Bhaskara tomorrow morning and talk to him. Get ready to leave by tomorrow afternoon. I'll arrange for a taxi.'

'Where to? What do you mean, get ready?'

Beads of perspiration glistened on Kumudhini's face.

'Where else? Am I dead? Do you think Bhaskara has been calling me Mavaiyya Mavaiyya for nothing?'

'I ... I don't know *what* you're talking about ...?'

'You women are all like this. Nothing enters your heads quickly. Do what I ask you to do.' Vasudevaraya deliberately spoke light-heartedly, intimately.

'No! No! I won't go with you! Please don't take me away from here.' Kumudhini cried out in alarm. Her hand caressed her womb without being aware of what it was doing. 'No! I won't come!'

'Magu, you don't have to get *so* frightened. It's better for you to come home. Don't stay here alone. You may come back here in four months ... with your baby.'

'No ... no ... no.' Kumudhini spoke softly as if to herself.

Sheena looked at Vasudevaraya as if to say, 'See! Didn't I tell you?' Vasudevaraya was quiet for a while. As for Kumudhini, she sank into a chair, her face veiled in anxiety and confusion.

'Magu, it's not wrong for you to be so scared. I can understand your fears. But set them aside for now. Don't think of me only as Bhaskara's Mavaiyya. Think of me as your father too.'

Kumudhini looked up at him. Countless thoughts were milling around in her head: 'Bhaskara used to say, "Those who considered themselves to be of a higher caste have trampled on those said to be of the lower castes in so many ways. Who knows how many years have to go by before we slough off the skin of caste and reveal our true humanity!" How is this man my father? From where? Does he think the feelings of a child will well up in me the moment he asks me to see him as my father? My father alone is my father. The others can only be equal to *him*. That's all. Will such a short time do for this man to become my father's equal?'

'... No, you can't trust me. And there's no point in me blaming you. Magu, it's normal for you to wonder why I've come all of a sudden to take you home. It's natural for you to be suspicious. But remember something. Whatever Bhaskara is doing now has been my dream. Though I'm nearing sixty, I've only been wallowing in a dream; I haven't made an effort to wake up and act. Bhaskara has done what I haven't. And this is the respect I show him; taking care of his wife when he can't. Your baby has to be born in my house. Let us admit you to a hospital for the birthing if need be. We'll take care of you after that. Bhaskara's wife is not a destitute.'

Kumudhini did not speak a word. To Sheena, she looked helpless. 'Athigay, think it over. There's no need to be so bewildered. Tell us how you feel about it tomorrow morning,' he said as he brought out two mats and pillows and said to his father, 'Come, Appayya. Let's sleep.'

Vasudevaraya was tired after the seven-hour journey. He went to the bathroom for a wash. When he came out Kumudhini said softly, 'Wait, I'll get you some milk....'

'I don't want milk, I don't want anything. If you'll come with us tomorrow, fine. Or else, I'll stay here putting off all the work I have to see to.' Kumudhini continued to sit, her chin resting on her hand.

By the time Sheena got up the next morning, Kumudhini had already made coffee. He brushed his teeth, had his coffee and said, 'Don't bother to make any breakfast, Athigay. I'll get something from the restaurant by the time Appaiyya wakes up.'

'I'm not tired. I'll make something. That's nothing much,' she said.

'Have you ever been tired?' he teased her. 'Let that be. Tell me, shall I get some idlis?'

'*Hoon.*'

By the time he rushed through his bath and brought the idlis, Vasudevaraya was already up and having his coffee.

'I couldn't sleep well,' he grumbled, 'Too many mosquitoes.'

'I too couldn't sleep well. My eyes are burning as if I sat up all night watching a play.'

'So, I was the only one who's slept well,' said Sheena.

The three of them were deliberately talking of this and that. No one talked of what they had discussed the previous night. It was getting to be nine. Then Vasudevaraya said, 'Come, let's go and see Bhaskara.'

'I'll come to see him but I won't come to *your* place.' Kumudhini tried to keep the anxiety of the previous night from her voice.

'What if Bhaskara agrees to send you?'

'I've made all arrangements here. Things will work out somehow. Don't worry about me.'

'Okay, Maharayithi! Come, let's go and see him.'

The three of them set out. As they went down the steps, quite a few pairs of eyes were peeping out of windows.

By the time they reached the prison, got permission from the authorities, and met Bhaskara, it was eleven.

'Oho, Bhaskararayaru! How are things in your Mavaiyya's house?' laughed Vasudevaraya.

'*You* must tell me, Mavaiyya,' Bhaskara retaliated in good humour with a serene smile.

'With a fully pregnant wife at home, why did you have to worry about the affairs of the town, Maharaya?' Though the words were his own, the way he spoke them was so much like Parthakka or Gowramma.

Bhaskara laughed.

'How're you?' he asked tenderly, looking at his wife. Kumudhini nodded to say she was fine.

'You stay here without worrying about her. I'll take her home.'

Bhaskara looked speechless for a moment. Recovering, he said, 'What did you say, Mavaiyya?'

'I said your wife's birthing will be in our house. We too have a maternity hospital in our town, in case you don't remember.'

'What is it you're saying, Mavaiyya? If she goes into that curdling ambience, won't it affect her?'

Vasudevaraya felt it was a slap in the face but he laughed heartily. 'You're something else, aren't you?' he said, 'I thought you'd be overjoyed; that you'd ask me if your mother and Gowrathe had consented to take her in; that you'd congratulate me for pulling it off. Look, even there you've seen my smallness. Now I'm utterly defeated.'

'Mavaiyya, don't take her. I don't want you to.'

'Maharaya, will it be okay if I bring your wife and child back safely? Her people aren't willing to take her home. Your neighbours don't even look your way. Of what use is a hospital? Will they look after her for the three months after birthing? I'm not dead yet. I mean, the dream in me isn't dead yet. When you're doing so much, let me do my bit too. Don't be so embittered, Bhaskara.'

Bhaskara did not say anything. He turned towards his wife. She stood leaning against a pole. When he looked at her she shook her head to say she did not want to go at all.

Seeing Bhaskara looking solemn, Vasudevaraya said, 'So it looks as if you don't trust me. You kept calling me Mavaiyya, Mavaiyya, and I presumed I could think of your wife as my daughter. But now you've made a public statement that I'm a worthless Mavaiyya. What a person you are, Bhaskara! And to think I thought of you differently! *I* need a whipping now! This shows you haven't yet entered that level of thought where the question of caste doesn't even enter your head. When I invite Kumudhini to my house, why should it occur to you that I belong to one caste and she to another? Now try and look beyond such things. I'm inviting her as a person. Will you send her? Or, shall I bind her hands and legs and load her into a taxi? Let's see what you can do being in prison.' Though Vasudevaraya started out seriously, he ended up teasing.

Bhaskara stood awhile staring at him. Then he turned towards his wife. She stood with her chin pressed against the pole as if she were dumb.

'Go with him,' he said to her, 'Caste does not dwell in everybody. Here and there, humaneness may live in some too. Don't be afraid.'

As soon as she heard that, Kumudhini started sobbing. Bhaskara stroked her head to comfort her, 'We shouldn't ever lose heart. Let's trust in humaneness once again. Go with Mavaiyya. Don't worry about me.'

'Fine, Maharaya! So you respect me at least this much. Not that you do. I wrested respect from you, didn't I? So, we'll go now. It's not nice for me to say I'm there for you if you need me. But I don't say things because they sound nice. I mean them. You have to let me know if you need me. Did you get everything ... everything I said? I may come back after leaving her at home. Just in case you need....'

Bhaskara cut him short, 'Don't *ever* do that. I'll send her only if you'll be with her until she returns.'

'So, you're hemming me in, are you? Fine! All right, don't worry.'

Bhaskara smiled his winsome smile. 'That's the Bhaskara I know,' thought Vasudevaraya, treasuring the smile. 'That smile is Bhaskara. When he smiles that way, there's no one as handsome as he.'

The husband and wife bade goodbye to each other with their eyes. Sheena stood apart from it all, taking everything in like a journalist as if he had to submit an accurate report of the proceedings.

fifteen

Another Birth

'I can't tell you a story tonight, Putta. I don't know why but my mind isn't working today,' Parthakka pleaded but Putta would not let her be. He had had his dinner and so he laid his head on her lap and pestered her to unravel a bit of the Ramayana before bedtime. The connections in Parthakka's story went haywire from time to time and Putta himself had to sort them out until, at last, his eyes glazed with sleep. Shami kept an ear tuned to Parthakka and Putta while doing her homework. Lying on her bed close by, Jaya watched Parthakka's mouth.

That was when they heard the sound of a horn.

Putta pricked up his ears, suddenly alert. As he heard a car stop, his sleep vanished.

'Car!' he exclaimed. Parthakka grew anxious.

'Mani, won't you get up?' she said brusquely. But even before he could, she quickly pushed his head off her lap and went into one of the inner rooms.

Saroja and Shiva stepped out. Shami ran to them forgetting to cover her pen. Jaya too joined them in a flash, tossing aside her coverlet.

Even as they gathered at the front door, pushing and shoving, Sheena and Vasudevaraya got out of the car. Kumudhini sat still, petrified.

'Get down, magu,' said Vasudevaraya, opening the door on her side for her. Gowramma had joined her children silently. 'Aha! Wonder how he fell for this dark-skinned woman!' she whispered, more for her own satisfaction. As soon as Saroja saw Kumudhini, she stepped forward but her mother caught the flesh on her arm in a painful twist.

'Get in!' she hissed softly as she went inside, 'Or else, I'll hack you down.'

Saroja walked forward, nevertheless, rubbing the arm where her mother had pinched her. 'Come in, Athigay,' she said, smiling. As the two stepped inside, the others followed them.

'Saroja, she may be tired. Give her something to drink. We can have dinner later,' said Vasudevaraya.

'Dinner will be a little late, anyway, Appaiyya. I'll make some white rice now; the boiled rice will take ages to cook. Did you tell us when you were coming?' Saroja asked her father laughing, and then to Kumudhini, 'Would you like to have a wash, Athigay? Come.' She was about to take her to the bathroom when her father said, 'Wait a bit,' and went in ahead of her. Seeing Gowramma peeping through a crack in the kitchen door, he said, 'Oho, you're still here, are you? I thought you'd gone to Koppa.' She looked like jwalamukhi.[1] He looked around. He could not see Parthakka anywhere. 'Make something for us to drink,' he said to his wife, 'Now don't start repeating the same things all over again.'

'Yes, I'm good enough only for cooking, aren't I? Do you need me for anything else? ... Now that you've brought her here?'

'What else? Have I been talking to you in English all this while? Didn't you understand what I said just now?'

Tears streamed down Gowramma's cheeks. 'What's the point in talking to him?' she thought, going towards the oven, 'He's always had his own way, hasn't he? This is, after all, my fate.' She could hear Vasudevaraya saying, 'Saroja, show her the bathroom. Give her the soap and a towel.' Her stomach churned.

Saroja mixed the coffee her mother made and served it to the three of them. 'Rice will be ready in half an hour,' she announced. 'There's curry and vegetables and everything else. There's also some cooked par-boiled rice. But it's just enough for one person. Anyway, we've already added a little water to it to keep it from getting spoilt.'

[1] jwalamukhi: volcano

'I'll have that now,' said Sheena, 'Slice an onion to go with it. There're the pickles, anyway. Mixed with buttermilk, it'll make a great meal. We can eat together after the rice is done.' It looked as if they were all making small talk deliberately to ward off the dense silence that threatened to envelop the house.

'Where's Parthakka?' said Vasudevaraya after his coffee.

'Who knows? She may be somewhere around,' replied Saroja. She spread a mat for Kumudhini, saying, 'Lie down for a while, Athigay. You must be tired after that long journey.'

Vasudevaraya became anxious when he could not see Parthakka anywhere. 'She was right here, Appaiyya,' said Putta, trying to be helpful, 'She was telling me a story and when we heard the car, she dropped my head, *dhudum,* on the mat and went inside. Look here, Appaiyya! See the bump I've got on my head.' But his Appaiyya had no time for him; he was much too worried about Parthakka. 'Look for her, makkale,' was all he said. But today the children could not heed their father's call. Each stood in a corner, staring at their big-bellied guest. Even Putta, who did not get the petting he expected from his father, stood there sucking his thumb, giving Kumudhini a lop-sided smile every time she looked at him.

Vasudevaraya went from room to room, looking everywhere with a rising sense of panic. But wherever he looked, he could not see Parthakka. *Arre*, where could she have disappeared so suddenly? He turned on the light outside and looked everywhere in the backyard. He peeped into the room where cattle-feed was cooked. On a vague suspicion, he even went to the well and peered in, listening intently for sounds. There were no signs of anything. He came inside. Wasn't the puja room with its flickering oil-lamps the only place he hadn't checked? He went inside. And there in that little room, Parthakka sat crouching behind the door as children do when playing hide and seek. She looked desperate.

Vasudevaraya sat beside her and said gently, softly, 'Your pregnant daughter-in-law has come home, Parthakka. Is this any way to behave? Get up, get up!'

'Never talk to me again. Think I'm dead from today. You've done a great thing, haven't you? Isn't that enough? You've brought a Korathi home without caring for consequences. You've made your house the

Koppa of the Koragas. You've ruined your *whole* family!' Her voice rose hysterically in anguish.

'Will you talk softly or not? What's on your mind? Do you wish to kill the unborn child? Is that it?'

'Vastheva! I asked you to get out of here, didn't I? You've even entered *God's* room! You who've touched *her*! Ayyo, Devare!' Parthakka trembled like one possessed.

Vasudevaraya spoke purposefully, 'Parthakka, if you talk this way, I'll bring her right into this room. What will you do then?'

'Before you bring her in, throw that saligrama out!'

'So, if I throw the saligrama out, I can bring her here, can I?' Vasudevaraya said, laughing deliberately to lighten the mood. And then he added seriously, 'Look here, Parthakka. If she cannot come into God's room, if the saligrama really cannot accept her, if *that* is the truth, then the saligrama should get up on its own and jump into the well, shouldn't it? Let's find out the truth right now.'

'This *must* be Kaliyuga for such things to happen. I don't need your nonsense. You've performed my funeral rites in bringing her here. You don't need to do it again when I die. Vastheva! Ayyo, Vastheva!' As Parthakka's voice rose to the skies, Vasudevaraya got up. Without being aware of it, he lost his patience, and said, 'I'll see what'll happen. If you're going to scream like this, I'll surely bring her here.'

'Ayyo, Maharaya, you won't stop at anything, however disgusting it may be,' said Parthakka, getting up and nimbly climbing the ladder to the dark attic in the room with an agility she had never known before.

It was cramped with many different things: a vessel of rice hapla; balls of tamarind pounded with salt and wrapped in dhoopa leaves to be preserved from worms; copper and brass cauldrons that came down only during celebrations like Mahalaya or a namakarana or an upanayana but otherwise sat there gaping, adding their darkness to the darkness of the attic.

Vasudevaraya had not expected this. He did not know what to do. He climbed after her shouting, 'Ayyo, Parthakka, careful! You may hurt yourself.... Hoi! Where're you going? Come down at once!' He stood on the highest rung and peered in. He could only see deeper darkness beyond the darkness; he could not see Parthakka. He wondered behind which of those cauldrons she could be hiding. What a calamity!

'Mani, Shiva!' he called out.

'What's it Appayya?' Shiva came running.

'Get a torch.'

Struck by the unusual sight of his father atop the ladder, Shiva stood like Thattiraya.

'This Parthakka is hiding somewhere over there. Go quickly, get a torch.'

Shiva laughed aloud. 'Not bad for her! Climbing up the ladder and sitting in the attic, all to feel she's above the rest of us, haan?' He ran off to get the torch.

As soon as Putta heard from Shiva that Parthakka had gone up to the attic and was sitting there, he ran into the puja room, pulled out his thumb from his mouth and shouted, 'Parthakka, there's a *bhoota*[2] in that darkness. It'll gobble you up! Ayyo, come down quickly!'

---

[2] bhoota—has two meanings: Ghost and the past. Both the meanings are relevant to the symbolic darkness that has swallowed Parthakka.

An Autobiographical Note

My desire is to achieve in my writing the balance I have heard about in the inner world of the home.

I was born and brought up in a large family though not a joint one. We were many children with kinsfolk and friends coming in every day and sometimes staying over. In a family like this, I got a close look at the beautiful and innocent lives of growing children, the mental confusions caused by living closely with others, problems and joys, gaiety, pain and sorrow. In those days, girls who used to study up to primary or middle school, or sometimes completed high school, had now begun to study further. So by the time I came along there was a college in Kundapura itself, and it was easier to obtain a college education. The situation of women around me at the time I was born was the situation of all women of that age; so I won't go into those details here. But I'll speak about what I saw, and what might lie within the experience of people like me. I don't need to add that all this nurtured my life as a writer.

For us (by which I mean girl children), staying indoors was a habit. This 'inside' was what you came to after crossing the courtyard and verandah. If there were menfolk sitting on the verandah, we did not go there. Truly, we had to think that this race of 'men' was cruel since we could not go where they were, and even in the daytime we could not go out unaccompanied. But funnily enough we never thought them cruel. How fortunate men were in that regard! There were even those who spoke approvingly about any girl who showed the 'courage' to move fearlessly where the men were. 'That girl is really brave. Not the slightest fear of men!' they would say. Such girls inspired as much fear as the men did. In the front room, the woman clients of my lawyer father huddled on a bench, or stood leaning against the grill. There were also women who spoke loudly and fearlessly to the lawyer. When we heard such a voice, we would peek out curiously: 'Who's that? Speaking loudly like a man?'

When I was young, girls did not sit on chairs. Only men occupied chairs, and read the newspaper thus seated. We sat on the floor to read and write. My oldest sister was considered very clever. The founder of the Hindu Elementary School, Headmaster Bantwal Raghunatharaaya, had had a desk-bench made for my sister, perhaps to encourage other girls to follow her example. There was only one such desk-bench in the schoolroom. It was there even when I went to school, much to my pride. Everyone wanted to sit on it, but it was the class toppers who were given that special honour. In a long essay of mine called *Through The Table and Chair* I have written about some of these experiences. When I was in school, a woman very close to my family came to teach there. Another woman who used to visit us often, and who frequently criticized people's behaviour, making fun of them, or pitying them, and passing her days in amusing herself this way, called me aside and said: 'So she's your teacher, ha? Then, she must be a big teacher indeed! I heard that she sits on a chair and farts with her ass in the air.' The woman couldn't stop laughing, and I stood there bewildered, reduced almost to tears as she laughed on and on.

We didn't go anywhere except to school, and back home, where we had many chores to occupy us. I say this with some bitter pride and not as a complaint. In the summer, not a ray of sunshine could be wasted. Rows and rows of mats, and spread on them to dry were rows and rows of *happala* and *sandige* (rice wafers). At night an elderly woman—either a widow known to the family or a poor relative—would pour innumerable *seers* of rice flour into a copper vessel, and knead the flour well with chili and salt and asafetida. The next day the flour was pounded with a wooden pestle before being shaped into whatever was required. There was no dearth of people to pound and cut and roll out. The rice papad making, in particular, occupied the entire day and night. Today's children will never know the folk pleasure of nibbling raw papad dough! In the kitchen, dangling from a beam would be strings of onions, and row upon row of yellow cucumber nestling in a noose of tender coconut palm. What importance is given to the sense of taste in the love of life! Matching that are the methods of collecting and preserving. Especially in the mango season there was not a second to spare. When we had work to do in all four directions, suddenly sometimes—like a ship foundering—kinfolk would descend upon us. It was a house where anyone could bring their friends and acquaintances, at any time, without any hesitation or anxiety, and they would get a joyous welcome. The serving of food, an 'always-readiness' to be hospitable, was the permanent feature of our inner world. There was never any feeling that it would make things difficult for us. For, what did we have except work and more work? Reading, writing, singing—all these came later. All around us were the conversations with people who came and went, with all kinds of small quarrels breaking out in the cracks between those words, fights, investigations, challenges; since my father was the eldest son, every ritual took place in our house: last rites, Mahalaya, the feast of Shravana, the pujas for Ganesha, family weddings, engagements, 'girl-seeing', *upanayana*—you name it! After every function, the inner house was filled with happiness and enthusiasm, with jokes, sulks, and small enmities—for all kinds of reasons. The whole house would turn topsy-turvy at such times. In such a family, living among children being born and growing up, was as though one had seen the whole world.

In the midst of birth, I said. At that time, we saw only that. The first death I saw was my father's end. This was also the first calamity that befell me. When I was born, my father was already past fifty. A lawyer by profession, he was a caring and loving man. With all of us shouting and screaming around him, never once did he scold or beat anyone. All he had to do was raise his voice a little and say: 'What's going on?' and we would disappear, humiliated. Father was a devout man, and had a special love for literature and music. He had a good collection of books in the house. When we opened the beautifully-bound Valmiki and Tulsi

Ramayana he read everyday, we were captivated by the pictures inside. They were brightly coloured, and printed on thick soft paper. Every day before supper he read at least one chapter. As he walked about, *shlokas* and *dohas* sprung melodiously from his lips. Having heard this as a child, to me no singer, no matter how famous, can match my father's voice. His clients who came at all odd hours were spoken to with great care, and by the time my father came indoors it was sometimes past eleven at night. Then he read his Ramayana, and after that ate his meal. My mother used to sit drowsily against a pillar in the dining hall, waiting. When I remember my father this is the picture of my mother that comes to mind too. Now when I think about it, I feel that my father had very old-fashioned views about women. If he had been here now, I would have asked him some important questions.

My mother was Father's second wife. She came from a moderately well-off agricultural family. When she came into the house, there were already five children. The oldest daughter was only a year younger than my mother. There were several children and adults who had come from the village to Kundapur to study or work, and they too lived in the house. In the middle of pregnancies and births, rebukes and criticisms, my mother saved her voice by clinging to unvarnished truths. Maybe because she came from a farmer's family, work was her *veda*. This is one of the legacies she left her children. When my father was alive, we never saw them have the slightest quarrel. Till today this is a matter for astonishment for me, and a lamp to show the way. My father himself used to say, 'She was a person without any pretence.' In her last days too, she remained like this, a woman who gave us all her boundless love. Never bowing to crookedness, she used arrogance to protect herself. A person true to herself, who all her life possessed an independent mind. Not someone you can understand easily. I came to understand her only after the 'stree' in me began to think. She should really have been a writer. Not only did her words have such a unique ring to them, strength, clarity, and reflectiveness but she also had a powerful critical intellect. Anything I write today is two per cent of what she might have written. Her easy skill in putting words together is something I cannot match even if I stand on my head. I have only one complaint against her. For a woman who valued work above everything else, it was a crime for a girl to sit reading as though the world was forgotten. On this she never compromised.

In those days the custom was to have weddings in the house itself. Although, in every December and January the courtyard was plastered with mud clay, this was done with even greater enthusiasm when an auspicious event was about to take place. Clay was brought in a cart. This had to be mixed with water, and then the men stamped it down with bare feet. The mud coated their legs like boots, and then they had to pound it with wooden pounders and make it hard and smooth. Although this was a man's job, there was a woman named Seethu amongst us who joined in the work. She would appoint two women servants as her assistants, and take part at every stage of the work, from the time the mud was shovelled out of the cart. Whose footprint was that on the half-dry clay? No one would answer. There, another footprint, of a little child. Next morning we would find the prints of dogs and cats. Did so much animal traffic pass through as we slept? All these marks had to be smoothed out before the final drying. Until late at night Seethu was at work with the smoothing stone (she appears in my story *Allallina Lokadavaru* as Manji), along with Chandu, Girija, and Seethu's old mother Sooru. The clay, which the first rains could spoil, could always do with more smoothing. As they worked with bowed heads, immersed in their task of smoothing the earth, they talked and sang. Of those who became pregnant, they whispered news of doubts and humiliations. In the songs the husband always went to the prostitute's house. The wife of the elder brother was always an ogress. We children used to join them in working on the yard. In those days when there was no radio or TV, we sucked in everything we saw and heard.

In my mother's house, there was a servant woman named Kamala. First she worked in the house, but as she got older she came only to milk the cows, and then only to sweep the verandah, doing the tasks she was still able to do. Every day without fail she wore flowers and kumkum, and walked with her head held high, her neck at a slant, swinging her arms. To this day if anyone asks her, 'Kamala, how're things with you?', she replies: 'What can I say? Twelve annas on my knee.' When she was young, her husband had gone away across the ghats. Kamala dedicated her entire life to the long labour of bringing up her only daughter.

These are stories you will find anywhere in the world. My purpose is not simply to tell this story. What was most surprising about Kamala was the poem she cradled within her. When we went home we would see Kamala chatting away and skipping as she sang. One of her songs went thus:

He said, girl ... girl
I said Yes?
The basket's in the boiler
He said girl ... girl.
I said Yes?

When she recited this poem the gaiety on her face was of a different quality. She didn't only recite this; she would stand up, skip around the yard, and chant the words. She swayed back and forth as though she sat in a musical swing. Whenever we saw her, we would say, 'Give us the poem—He said girl ... girl ...', and she would say 'O, burn that'. But even as she said it, she began to recite the words. It was as though the whole world was hidden in the different nuances of this poem. The world of women in my writings lies here: 'He said girl ... girl, I said yes?' in the rise and fall of these voices, in their sway and their softness.

And so I grew, watching women like Kamala, Krishni, Seethu, and others, those without husbands, those whose husbands were barely there, husbands who had gone away over the ghats and started another family, husbands who descended from the heavens to join the family but who could disappear at any moment. All these women lived amidst sorrow and poverty, but they were strong. They overcame their helplessness in their own ways and took heart so they could live. For a long time I thought that through her poem Kamala was weaving a dream of conjugal happiness. One day suddenly I had a doubt and so I asked her: 'Who's the 'he' who calls out to you?' Without answering, she began to giggle, and quickly moved away. Only then did I begin to glimpse the different layers of the song. From that day on, our Kamala was even closer to my heart.

As I write I remember all these women once more and my eyes grow moist. If I try to describe my companionship with the servant women, the way we used to work together (even if I was scolded by the elders), the cows and buffalos, their calving, the antics of the calves, the lazy beauty of the cows, the pestering of the Haiguli god, the offerings of fruit and coconut.... I could fill many pages with this. If I stepped into the cowshed, I lost myself in that world. Now it's all like a dream....

I remember also a woman called Varija. Her husband felt humiliated by her raising her head and singing at every wedding and *munji* and threatened to throw her out of the house if she ever sang again. She never did.

If you came into the closed verandah where my father had his legal practice, you would see the women petitioners there. Scared, huddled, neither sitting nor standing. There were Brahmin women among them too. They were all there for maintenance disputes; hapless women whose very maintenance had been threatened and who had found someone who helped them to file a petition. With them were the men who had come to provide explanations. Along with this picture was that of the modern women. There were women in our town who were at least twenty years ahead of their time. They would come by themselves to discuss their cases with my father. 'Mr Hebbar' was how they addressed him. They appeared to have flown in over the heads of the fearful illiterate women huddling on the verandah. Seated on chairs right opposite my father, they would conduct their business in English. Their walk, their speech, their clothes—all exuded self-confidence. It served to frighten the huddled women even more. When we heard the voice of a modern woman we too would peep out. We would go and tell the older women at home, and they too would look out quietly from the window's edge, saying: 'Look at that, speaking loudly like a man. Popping English words too.' What surprises me is that even as we stared in astonishment at those women's behaviour, they finished their business and walked away rapidly, without sparing a glance for the other women petitioners huddled on the verandah. Today this picture provides me with different meanings than it did then. For instance: in those days, it was exceptional for a girl to study upto the eighth standard. My older sisters had studied until the tenth. I went to college too. Did all that learning really make us more aware of the world around us? I only see the creation of a class of educated women set apart from those who did not go to school, even within our women's world.

How did I learn poetry? Among my lessons would be the *pandal* thatch made from woven coconut palm leaves. That was truly a poem. Through the hundred crevices of the thatch, the sun would peep inside, leaning on his stick. We thought we could climb to the skies on the rays of sunshine. And the stick—we couldn't grasp it. All over the floor were rings of light. The midday sun traced *rangoli* patterns; inside the house was the cool darkness. We played games between the pillars. If anyone can catch these in words, she would become Brahma, no doubt! (Brahma having no gender.) Unawares, we breathed in these experiences.

The pandal rises. The procession draws near. The bridegroom stands, like Rama holding his bow—dressed in dhoti and chest-cloth and necklace, holding his *dantu kolu*. Inside, the bride, seated like a tempest. She comes to the *mantapa*, head lowered like a culprit. This mantapa was fashioned by Uncle Vachanna just the day before. He had worked the whole night knocking tiny nails with a tiny hammer into the frame, to hold the strips of *zari* and the flowers covered with gold dust, to make the mantapa look like Amaravathi's. This image had lain deep in my memory. How it comes up before me now!

Uncle would build the mantapa. We girl-children would watch. As we watched we entered the mantapa one by one. When we came out of it, we were two. We were separate from the house now, ready to leave. This house, this yard, the wall, the kitchen, the grinding stone, the churning stick, the well, the cradle, little baby brother, the attic, the cowshed, sisters, older brothers—leaving all these behind, even the pit in the backyard where the placenta was buried with the umbilical cord ... Then one didn't feel the pain. Now, one is filled with the raw pain of the cord tugging.

The procession goes back. One person less in the house. Only one person, but it feels as though many people have gone away. After the wedding, in the midst of sweets and savouries and seeing off relatives, there is the sense of emptiness. There is a cry that hasn't been uttered. The umbilical cord is burning. In Amma's face, in Father's steps. Departing and meeting, life's long braiding together. From this pain and joy springs poetry. From this the world comes to life.

In those days or even now, the main question raised amongst our people is: 'How much gold will you put on the bride?' Once upon a time the eligibility of a groom was measured by his inheritance; slowly this criterion changed to one of education and employability. It has always astonished me that the family of a wealthy bride looked for an educated groom, and the family of an educated groom expected a rich bride. This hasn't changed over the years. A rich hotel owner from Bangalore married off his daughter at a tender age to a village near ours, just because the groom was a 'double graduate', and I saw the girl learn with great difficulty to live with her chores, the cowshed, buffalos, and cowdung; a life she had not seen even in her dreams. There was not even the hint of a smile on her face. To this day I search her face and there is nothing. It makes me desperate to think that even an educated woman's eligibility is measured by the gold she brings.

In those days Brahmin widows were everywhere, with shaven heads and red saris. I will give an example to show how they were accustomed to their own cruel life and how it seemed so unexceptional to us. There was a cook in our house, a widow from my grandmother's family. A short, buck-toothed, knock-kneed woman; known for her sturdiness. A woman with three daughters whose husband had died. She was sent to help out during one of my mother's pregnancies. I have written about her peculiar personality in *Ondu Aparadha Tanikhe* (Inquiry into a Crime). Every month the barber who came to the house used to shave her head. When she heard that the barber had come, she would go straight to him. We watched in amusement as her hair fell in clumps and the skull got smoother. In five minutes it would all be over, and she would rise as if from a completed chore. We used to amuse ourselves looking at her bald head. 'Show, show', we would plead, and she would whip her sari's edge from her head and laugh. We would pass our hands over the prickly scalp and giggle, saying 'Like a ball of wet dough.' She behaved as though it was all very natural. Once in a while, during Amavasya or Full Moon or at any old time she would become possessed. Then she would drink a whole vessel of water, roaring loudly. For this too there was no small audience. We used to leave all our games and come to watch her. The spirit would leave her only if she was given a plug of tobacco. If a bunch of betel leaves and some tobacco wasn't brought from the market for her, the spectacle would become worse. The widow would disappear into the hay room or the coconut attic, and refuse all food.

Mother had to accomplish the feat of wooing her back. Once she came out, however, she only thought of work. No one had the heart to send her away, since she was quite destitute. Once in my older sister's house, there was a puja for Sridhara Swamigalu. The widow was taken there so that he could bring her out of her sickness. The Swami sprinkled holy water on her and said: 'Away, go away.' He pressed her foot with his big toe. Then the spirit bellowed, saying he was one who had died by water. The Swami gently told him to go away to his ashram, where the Swami would look after him. The spirit bellowed again. The widow fell in a swoon. But after this she stopped being possessed. But she still climbed into the attic in rage and sulked from time to time. They say that it was her husband's brother, who had died an untimely death, who used to 'possess' her. The widow lived with us till she died, her death being one of the big upheavals in my young life. How many women there were like her in those days! In my maternal grandfather's house too an old woman lived on in this fashion. As though half-crazed. All these experiences went into my story, *Akku*.

Of the cook's daughters, the eldest was unbeatable for her weak, helpless, lazy, and incompetent state, and the youngest for being stubborn, rough and steadfast. The middle one, who was perfectly happy to be submissive, was the only one who became a part of the social mainstream. Even today I see before me the picture of the older one, pregnant, knocking at our back door, her face and feet swollen.

Then there were others who became part of the family, who we held in warm regard instead of the grandmother we had never known. In my novel, *Asprushyaru* (Untouchables) there is a depiction of one such woman. They completed their years without a sound, leading perfectly blameless lives, as though they had changed the meaning of happiness to suit the age's definition of 'respectability.' Without ever listening to themselves, they ended their days.

Another woman who had earned the reputation of being strong-willed was a doctor's wife who drove a car. We would stare at her as she drove past, the husband sitting beside her. She would drive the car alone too. If her husband rode a motorbike, she would sit on the pillion with her hand on his shoulder. All this was new to us. And above everything else, she spoke English! How all the men too respected her! I've written out my astonishment in *Through The Table and Chair*. The women made nasty comments about the doctor's wife, but were all respect when they faced her. She used to go to her husband's clinic and help out with the compounding. And would she come there like an ordinary woman? 'Most fashionably dressed', 'Wearing lipstick-gipstick', 'Wearing a starched sari'—that was her. She sat on a chair in the clinic, one leg thrown over the other, shaking the leg slightly, chatting away with the men who came there, laughing 'Ho ho ho' like a man, said the stories woven around her. She was like that till the day she died, which was only recently.

She remains clearly etched in my memory, maybe because I saw in her so many years ago the opening up of women to a new world of equality, and because she seemed to embody some of its confusions and transformations.

In the compound next to my house, there was a row of rented houses. In them lived for many years some devadasi women from Basrur. There was also a prostitute who lived there. This is the inspiration for my story *Chandale*. The girl children of the kalavantha went to school. The older ones had got jobs in offices. There was great friendliness between our house and that of those women. They had loud voices which didn't hush even when men were around. In their quarrels, their financial worries, their pregnancies and deliveries, they veered toward respectability in their conduct. The female kinfolk who visited them had been exposed to modern life. They used to visit us and partake of our hospitality. But they wouldn't come too far inside. They sat on the verandah or at the most came into the room just inside. In their talk there was easy mention of the men who 'kept' their elders. Speaking without any hesitation, they crossed over into a new life—a sight it was my good fortune to see. Witness to a social transformation.

As the girls studied to whatever level the times permitted, and then got married, the boys went away to Mangalore or Madras to study. They used to come home for the holidays, and we felt they had reached heights we would never attain. We treated them with a mixture of fear and respect. My eldest brother studied literature, and became a lecturer in a college for a while. When he came home, it was as though all the English dramatists and poets came with him. In the dining area, he would declaim from English plays, and we would gaze at him open-mouthed. We couldn't understand any of it from the words, but sought to make sense from his intonation and gestures. For a woman of the house to speak English was considered a mark of arrogance, 'Look at that one, flipping out her English words'—this criticism was made of all girls who tried to introduce English into their speech. The second brother was a great reader, and the third was a writer. It was his writings that first drew me to the act of writing. He gave the lie to the idea that writers were people who lived at a great distance from us. If my brother, so close, could do this, why not I? And so it happened. One day my second older brother scolded me for some reason. I felt humiliated, and the sorrow welled up in me. It wasn't a big enough thing to bring up with my father. My mother wouldn't have time to listen. (Have you noticed how one feels one can go to mother with a small problem but you need a big one to approach father?) And in any case she might take my brother's side. Where to store my sorrow then? The girl in me walked straight upstairs. Wrote and wrote as she sobbed. She wrote: What is justice? When will justice be done? She wrote in her own Kannada. She left it as it lay, covered with another sheet, and the same brother discovered it soon after and read it out loud and the girl felt as though she wanted the earth to open and swallow her up ... these memories still sparkle in my mind. That sheet of paper was lost. The quarrel was made up.

The life that grows amidst many others can also be a lonely one. It's only when I started to write, and write seriously, that I became aware of my loneliness, my confusions, my predicaments. Before that I imitated what I read, in copycat style, and copycat images. As for readers, the question never came up as to whom I was writing for. It's only when a reader rose up within me that my writing turned serious.

For the reader in me to hear and criticise all I said, I had to get married and leave my house, and stand right in the midst of life. Marriage was an event that woke me from slumber. I swear to you that even though I grew up amidst births and pregnancies, and although I heard whispers about it all the time, I had no idea how one got pregnant or gave birth. I knew the talk, but I had no knowledge. I thought that to know or read about all that was to be 'soiled.' So I came away from my house, pretending to know everything but actually quite innocent. Life in my in-laws' house sobered me up, increased my looking inward, and created in me the need to write. By then I had two children, and they saved my days from going completely to ruin. I enjoyed to the full, two pregnancies and the pleasure of children. I say to this day that this has remained one of the finest pleasures of my life.

In those days after marriage I was like a calf lost in the jungle. What I used to write at that time had no relation to my state of mind, but was just a strategy designed to help me forget my tribulations. Fortunately for me, my father-in-law treated me like a favourite granddaughter, with love and esteem, filling me with self-confidence. My husband, a good man among good men, took me to watch plays, listen to music and to literary gatherings, opening up a new world for me. Whenever I felt depressed, he alerted me to the fact that I was a writer. This was a real necessity for one who came from the kind of background I did.

In this way, staying basically inside the house, for the most part with women only, experiencing directly or indirectly all their sufferings, cruelty, and mutual torture, I attached myself to the world of writing. Through my work I sought to investigate the root causes of many things. I set forth to find out and give testimony regarding what the social predicament of women could do to them. My desire is to capture life without forgetting any of this.

I must also mention here another word from the world of women, from *streeloka*. It's a word I used to hear from my mother, *hadha*, balance. Bringing about a balance. It was perhaps her prayer-bead chant. Too much laughter or too much sorrow evoked from her the sharp scolding response that everything had to have a measure or balance. While chopping vegetables in the kitchen, while adding each spice, while checking how much cooking each dish required, and how much seasoning—if the 'balance' slipped, it was a job badly done. This balance was not something which could be measured, not something clearly defined. Each person had to find the appropriate balance. This concept of balance we have in India is to be found more in our kitchens and the inner life of our homes than in the lives of sages. My desire is to achieve in my writing, the balance I have heard about in the inner world of the home. Today if we women writers lose that balance, we slip into emotionality or rant and self-pity. Or we go in another direction, our words lending themselves to anger, rage and despair. To sway to either extreme is to acknowledge defeat.

For me, the world of women is one of Zen. We are not a group which can run away to the Himalayas. We continue living amidst the confusions and quarrels, the love and trust, of daily life. What is important to us is not whether the world is the truth or a lie. But work, work, and more work. We are a generation that reads and writes and sings and thinks and meditates, in the midst of work.

Although I don't have many illusions about writing, I can say without any hesitation that it strengthens what the world needs, the power to comprehend life, to save love from growing bitter; it strengthens our power to desire this, as well as our self-confidence. In the final analysis, it's a struggle to guard the flame of love's lamp from being extinguished by evil winds.

—Translated by Tejaswini Niranjana

Glossary

Aanegudde Ganapathi	The Vinayaka or Ganapathi temple is one of the oldest in Aanegudde (Udupi district). It is believed that Ganapathi, the son of Parvathi and Shiva, solves every problem.
Achyuthaashtaka	a litany of eight stanzas in praise to Krishna
adharmic	that which is against dharma; unrighteous
Agoli Manjanna	a hero of Tulu folk literature, the Bheema of Tulunadu.
amavasya	the new moon
amavasya boodhi	the day before the new moon, both the days are considered inauspicious as the nights are dark
anna	old Indian currency; 1/16 of a rupee
arathi	ritual of waving the sacred light before a god or a person
ashanaartha	maintenance
avatara	incarnation
Ayyo devare!	O god!
bairasa	towel
bajji	sliced vegetables, dipped in gram flour paste and deep-fried
beedi	country cigarette
baje-benne	a paste of nutmeg in butter

GLOSSARY

bimbala	a tree that bears sour fruit
Brahmarakshasi	a she-demon
Chandala	of the grave-digger community
chapaati	flat bread generally made with unleavened wheat flour
Chathurthi	fourth day after the new moon and full moon; here it is, feast of Ganesha Chathurthi, the feast of Ganesh, the son of Parvathi
Devadharu	deodar
dharma	duty, responsibility, righteousness
dhavani	a half-sari or a long veil worn over a skirt and blouse
dhobi	washerman
dosay	an Indian snack, pancake made from a watery batter of rice and lentil
Draupadi Vasthraapaharana	reference to Dushashana stripping Draupadi in court and Krishna coming to her rescue when she called on him (Mahabharata)
enjalu	spittle, considered ritually unclean
Ganesha Chathurthi	fourth day after the new moon in the month of Bhadrapada; the feast of Ganesha, the son of Parvathi and Shiva
Ganga Bhavani	tears; hyperbolic reference to Godess Ganga, the river in north India
ganji	gruel made with boiled rice
Gayathri Japa	taken from a hymn of the Rigveda (3.62.10), this mantra is an important part of the upanayana, an intiation ceremony for young Hindu boys. It is recited by Brahmin men as part of daily ritual. The prayer can be translated as, 'May the Almighty God illuminate our intellect to lead us along the righteous path.'
genda	a large pit filled with burning coal on which people walk to fulfil vows
gerasi	winnowing fan. A newborn is placed in it as it is considered ritually clean

happala	sun-dried crispies
Hosilajji	the threshold—granny
jaggery	molasses
janivaara	sacred thread a Brahmin wears as a sign of his commitment to a dharmic Vedic way of life
Jeerige kashaya	brew of cumin seeds
Jyeshta	onset of monsoon
kachche-panchche	a formal way of wearing the dhothi, taking the edge between the legs and tucking it in at the back at the waist
kadabu	thick batter of rice and lentil known as uddhina bele steamed in a cup-shaped mould
Kaliyuga	according to Hindu cosmology there are four yugas, each displaying a decrease in virtue and righteousness. The age of Kali is the worst and last
Kanva rishi	the sage who found the baby, Shakuntala, abandoned by her parents, and brought her up in his hermitage. Kalidasa has immortalized this myth in his play, *Abhijnanashakuntalam*
karma	Fate, destiny
kasa	after-birth
kasturi	musk
kela kone	a small room attached to the bathroom, used for oil massage
Kodi Koteshwara	Kodi festival of Koleshwara
Koosa	one of the lower classes of the outcastes
Koraga	the lowest of the lowest caste, cleaners of latrines, Korathi, a Koraga woman
kumkuma	a dot of sanctified red powder that Hindus put between the eyebrows; a widow has to give up this auspicious practice
madi, mylige	ritual purity and pollution
madhuve	the wedding ceremony
mantapa	dais on which the wedding ceremony is performed

mantras	vedic chants; power generated by the recitation of a word or words
Margashira or *Bhaarath*	December, winter, the genda ritual
maya	illusion
midbai	midwife
modaka	steamed dumplings with a sweet filling
Moksha	liberation from the cycle of birth
mundu	a length of cloth worn round the waist by men to cover the lower part of the body
munduga leaves	palm-like thorny leaves pinned to form a cup-like mould for steaming kadabu, a delicacy
muthaide	married woman whose husband is living
naivedya	food offered to the gods
namakarana	naming ceremony
nataka	play, drama
paapa	sin, wicked deeds. Also means 'poor thing!'
Paathaala	the lowest of the seven underworlds
Paathri	the man who takes on the persona of demi-gods. Here, of Kodiamma or the spirit of Kodi whenever she enters him
pachadi	vegetable salad
panchagavya	five items from the cow (milk, curd, ghee, urine, and dung) sipped as a ritual of purification
Parashurama	Parashu = hatchet, axe. Parashurama = Rama of the axe. He is the sixth avatara of Vishnu and the son of Jamadagni and Renuka. Shiva gifted him an axe. This is a reference to the way Parashurama, as an obedient child, chopped off his mother's head with one blow at his father's command.
pathrode	a popular delicacy made from steaming rolls of Pathrode or colocasia leaves smeared with a masala.
payasa	a sweet dish
pradhana devathe	presiding deity, used sarcastically here to mean money

prasada	food consecrated by the gods, given to devotees
puje	ritual worship
punya	virtue, good deeds
Ramayana	an epic: Dasharatha, King of Ayodhya, had three wives, Kausalye, Kaikeyi and Sumithre, and four sons. Rama, son of Kausalye, was the eldest. Bharatha was the son of Kaikeyi, Dasharatha's favourite wife. Lakshmana and Shatrugna were twins, sons of Sumithre, the third wife. Kaikeyi wanted her son, Bharatha to be king. Rama was banished to a forest for fourteen years. Seethe and Lakshmana went with him. Seethe was abducted by Ravana, a demon king....
rangoli	decorative designs drawn on the floor
Saligrama	Stones of the ammonite fossil recovered from the Gandaki river bed in Nepal. They are considered very sacred by conservative Brahmin families
sambara creeper	a medicinal herb
sanjay malligay	flowers of many colours that bloom only in the evening
sanyasi	renunciate
sashtipurthi or *shashtyabhdhipurthi*	a celebration of a householder's sixtieth birthday for the renewal of marriage vows as he enters another phase of life with his wife
seer	old Indian measure
shaavige	vermicelli
Shani	the planet Saturn, believed to have a malignant influence on one's life. So a problematic person is referred to as shani whose presence is bad luck
Shraddha	ritual for the death anniversary of a person
Shravana	the most auspicious month
Shudra	last in the list of four castes
sovereign	8 grams of gold
sunna	quicklime

suttu-maddu	herbal medicine
swathantrya	Independence
thakka-thaiya	rhythm of dancing feet
thattiraya	scarecrow
theertha	sanctified water
thorana	festoons on the main door
thoti	cleaner of latrines, and of the Koraga community
thumbe	a medicinal plant considered sacred and used in puje and other rituals
triloka sundari	beauty of the three worlds
udhinahittu	blackgram flour
ududhaara	string worn round the waist; loin string
unde	sweet specially made when a girl comes of age
upanayana	an initiation rite to confirm a Brahmin boy into the dharmic, Vedic way of life
Vaishaka	summer
Varunadeva	rain god
Vastheva	mispronunciation of Vasudeva
vatu	Brahmin boy
vedaparaayana	reading of the sacred scriptures